TRICK OR TRUCE

KRISTEN GRANATA

Copyright © 2023 Kristen Granata
All rights reserved.
www.kristengranata.com

No part of this book may be reproduced or transmitted in any form or by any means, electronic or mechanical, including photocopying, recording, or other electronic or mechanical methods, without the written permission of the author, except in the case of brief quotations embodied in a book review.

This book is a work of fiction. Names, characters, places, and incidents are either products of the author's imagination or are used fictitiously. Any resemblance to actual persons, living or dead, events or locales is entirely coincidental.

Editing & Formatting by My Brother's Editor

A NOTE FROM THE AUTHOR

As always, I used sensitivity readers for this story.

The heroine is unable to have children, and discusses it several times. This subject may be triggering for some, but please know that it has been written with the utmost care.

1

ELENA

"Trick or Treat?"

I balance the candy bowl on my hip as I prop open the door with my foot. "Wow, it's Spider-Man. I've always wanted to meet a real superhero."

The barely three-foot-tall Spider-Man standing on my porch lifts his mask, revealing his toothy grin. "Hi, Miss Lenny. It's me."

I feign a shocked gasp. "Oh, my god. Jake, it's you. I totally thought you were Spider-Man."

"No, you didn't. Spider-Man is much taller." He jerks his thumb over his shoulder. "Plus, my mom's standing right there."

I tilt my head, sizing him up. "Maybe it's the costume, but you do seem taller today."

His chest puffs out as he beams. "Really?"

"Definitely."

He gestures to my costume. "Are you Black Widow?"

"I sure am. We should team up and fight crime."

"Okay, but I have to be in bed by nine. Mom's letting me stay up a little later since it's a Friday."

"That's reasonable. I can take the second watch."

He thrusts his open bag at me. "Can I have extra Swedish Fish, please?"

"Jake!" Val slaps her palm on her chest. "I am so sorry. He must have forgotten his manners."

I dig out three mini-bags of Swedish Fish. "He said *please*."

She shakes her head. "He practically walked inside and invited himself to dinner at the last house."

Jake rolls his eyes. "They had a dog, Mom. I *had* to pet her."

"Of course, because that makes it okay. God forbid a kidnapper ever has a dog. You'd be a goner." Val shoots her son a glare before she turns back to me and smiles. "You look fantastic."

"Thank you. My friend decided to have her bachelorette party on Halloween, so we're going all-out with costumes this year."

"Take lots of pictures. I barely remember my bachelorette, but my friend has some compromising pictures of me on stage at a male review that she still uses as blackmail."

Jake hops off the top step, spraying fake webbing from his wrist. "What's a male review?"

"Nothing. Don't repeat that to your father."

I stifle a laugh. "Well, don't forget to brush your teeth tonight, Spider-Man. Superheroes can't get cavities."

"I don't see what the big deal is." Jake gives me a dubious look that's way beyond his eight years. "Baby teeth fall out. Who cares if we brush them? Seems like a waste of time to me."

"You've got a point, kid."

"He'll make a fantastic lawyer someday." Val holds out her hand for Jake. "Bye, Len. Have fun tonight—and have some extra fun for me."

I shoot her a wink. "You got it."

"Bye." Jake waves. "Have fun at your male review, whatever that means."

"See ya, Spider-Man. Catch some bad guys."

I head back inside my house and scribble a quick note onto a white piece of paper: *Happy Halloween. Take 2 pieces of candy!* I prop up the note behind the bowl of candy on the rocking chair on my porch so I can finish getting ready for my night out without any interruptions.

After I put the final touches on my hair and makeup, I gather all the bachelorette essentials—penis lollipops, a crown for the bride-to-be, and a few games—and toss them into a large tote. Then I grab my purse off the entryway table and balance the tray of pregame Jell-O shots as I step outside.

A flash of long dark hair flies off the top step of my porch and runs across my lawn, with four more girls following behind her.

"What the...?" I glance down at my rocking chair and my jaw drops open.

No candy.

No bowl.

Nothing but my note left behind.

They stole my candy bowl!

Without thinking, I drop my bags and lay the tray on the porch, and bolt after the group of girls. "Hey, come back here."

The thief holding my bowl glances over her shoulder, giving me a clear view of her face. She lives in the house directly across the street from me, but I don't know her name.

"I know where you live!" My eyes narrow. "Give me back my bowl."

But the girls pick up speed and widen the gap between us.

Trick-or-treaters jump onto the grass, clearing the path for us on the sidewalk as we barrel down the block.

"Somebody stop them!" I point in their direction. "They stole my candy."

I look like a lunatic—a grown adult flailing and shouting through the neighborhood, half-running, half-limping in my thigh-high stiletto boots as I gasp for air.

I can't keep this up for much longer.

"You can keep the candy," I offer. "I just want my bowl back."

If they're that hard-up for sweets, they can have it all. But the ceramic bowl, hand-painted with black cats and dangling spiders around an orange background, belonged to my nana.

I follow the girls for as long as I can until they turn a corner and disappear through someone's backyard. My lungs are burning. I'll never catch up to them at this rate, and I'm not about to climb a fence in this ridiculous outfit.

My feet slow to a stop, and I hunch over, resting my hands on my knees as I suck in big gulps of air.

Defeat mixes with anger, churning in my stomach like the perfect storm. What is wrong with kids today? I'd never have done something like that growing up—mainly out of fear that my parents would find out and beat my ass. Clearly, these girls don't have that same fear. Maybe they assume they won't get caught.

Fine. You want to be a punk-ass kid and steal my shit?

I'm telling.

I spin around with clenched fists, stomping my heels in the opposite direction toward the gray colonial house across the street from mine.

But my fury dies down the closer I get.

I've never formally met my neighbor. I don't even know his name. He keeps to himself and doesn't mingle with any of the families on our block. He cuts his lawn with earbuds in and checks his mailbox with his head down. Not the friendliest of people, but Lord, is he beautiful to look at.

I may or may not have checked him out…several times over the last few years.

I blow out a breath and get my head right.

I can do this. He's just a man.

A big, gorgeous, grumpy man who scowls so hard it looks like it hurts.

Still, just a man—whose bratty daughter just stole my bowl. I have every right to tell him what happened. He'll probably be mortified that his daughter did such a terrible thing and apologize.

Piece of cake.

I march up the porch steps and square my shoulders before ringing the doorbell, digging deep and hoping to find some untapped courage stored up inside me.

I'm Black *motherfucking* Widow. I don't get intimidated by men.

Until the door swings open, and I feel about the size of a literal black widow compared to the large man towering over me. His jeans are covered in dirt. His broad shoulders and thick biceps stretch his white T-shirt across his chest that's streaked with the same stains as on his pants. His skin is covered in a sheen of sweat, and strands of his dark hair stick up in every direction. Everything about him is rugged and tough-looking in every way—but it's nothing compared to his scowl. Overgrown scruff surrounds his frowning lips, with wiry gray hairs peppered into his beard. His pinched eyebrows create a dark hood over his obsidian eyes.

Give him an axe and a log to chop, and he'd have millions of followers on social media.

"H-hi, I'm Lenny. I live across the street." I jerk my thumb over my shoulder. "That white house right over there."

His dark eyes narrow to suspicious slits. "What can I do for you?"

Anxiety twists my stomach, so I blurt out the words before I lose my nerve. "Your daughter and her friends just stole my candy bowl off my porch. I caught her running away with my bowl in her hands. I chased her down the block but they were too fast and"—I let out a nervous laugh—"I mean, Jesus, are they Olympic runners or something? Not that I'm in the best attire for a high-speed chase. Some boots might be made for walking, but these heels are definitely not what you want to be wearing in a foot race, you know what I'm saying? No, of course you don't know what I'm saying. You don't wear heels. Unless you do, which is totally fine with me. I don't judge."

He doesn't laugh or crack a smile. Not even a humored grunt.

Ergo my nervous rambling continues.

"Anyway, the girls ran into someone's backyard and I lost them. And it's not so much about the candy—even though I was looking forward to a Sour Patch Kids-induced coma later tonight; the watermelon kind, because they're obviously superior—but it's the bowl. I just want the bowl back."

The man tilts his head the slightest bit, staring at me as if I'm an alien from Mars speaking another language. "So, you came here to accuse my daughter of stealing."

My chin jerks back. "It's not a false accusation, sir."

Sir? Why did I call him sir?

He crosses his arms over his chest, making his muscles appear even bigger as they bunch up around him. "Do you have proof?"

"Yeah, I saw her with my own two eyes."

He scoffs. "That's not proof."

I let out a frustrated breath and try to level with him. "Look, the candy bowl was my grandmother's. I kept it after she passed last year, and it means something to me. I truly don't care about the candy. Your daughter can have all of it. But I want the bowl."

"If it was so valuable, why would you leave it outside?"

My mouth drops open and anger boils in the pit of my stomach. Is he seriously blaming me for his daughter making the choice to steal?

I deal with parents like this all the time at school. They're all *not my kid*.

"You're victim shaming, you know that?" I let out an incredulous laugh. "You're exactly the kind of parent that's wrong with today's world, taking your child's side instead of reprimanding her for her actions."

"How I reprimand my daughter is none of your business."

"It is when she steals *my* property."

"If you think I'm going to believe you over her, you've got another thing coming."

"No, you have another thing coming."

Why did I just say that? What does that even mean?

One of his thick eyebrows pops. "Is that a threat?"

"Yeah, maybe it is."

His eyes bore into mine, and I squirm like a bug under a magnifying glass on a hot summer day.

But I'm not backing down.

I push up onto my tippy-toes and give him my best glare. "I want my candy bowl back…or else."

And then I spin around on my heels and strut away from him, holding my head high (and pray I don't trip and ruin my badass walking scene).

When I get to my house, I don't look back as I grab my bags off my porch and hop in my car. If I knew how to peel out, I'd do that too for good measure. Instead, I blast Metallica and rage-sing until I arrive at my best friend's house fifteen minutes later.

"The shots have arrived!"

Simone rushes toward me and wraps me in a bear hug. "Finally. What took you so long?"

"I'll explain later." I set the tray of shots on the coffee table and dig out the pink feathery crown from my tote. "First things first: You need your crown."

Simone squats down and tips her head while I pin the crown to her hair. "Wow, is this what you see down here? It's like a whole different world."

I give her a playful smack on her arm. "Screw you. Not everyone can be five foot ten and have curves like Beyoncé."

"Truth." She stands to her full height and plants her hands on her hips. "Now tell me what's wrong."

"Nothing's wrong."

"Lie."

Our friend Fatima bounces onto the couch and unwraps a Jell-O shot. "You're never late. Something had to happen."

I let out a groan and drop onto the cushion beside her. "You know my neighbor that lives across the street?"

"Hot Neighbor?" Simone gulps down a cup of red gelatin and sets the empty cup on the table. "The broody one you always talk about?"

As much as I hate to admit it now, I have mentioned him a few times. If a tall, dark, and handsome man lives across the street, you tell your best friend—especially when he's outside in a tank top cutting the grass, and there's no sign of a woman living with him.

But that was before I learned what an asshole he is.

"I don't always talk about him. But yes, for the purpose of this story, he's the neighbor I've told you about." I reach into my tote again and pull out the bag of penis lollipops, unwrapping one and sticking it in my mouth. "His daughter stole my candy bowl right off my porch. I saw her take it."

Fatima gasps. "Are you kidding? They took the bowl too?"

"Yup. So, I chased after them."

"In *those* heels?" Simone snorts. "You can barely walk without tripping. How did you manage that?"

"I tried my best, thank you very much, but I lost them. So, I went to her house and told her father, figuring maybe he'd be able to get the bowl back for me." My nose scrunches. "But Hot Neighbor turned out to be a giant dickhead."

Simone takes another shot as she sandwiches me between her and Fatima on the couch. "What did he say exactly?"

I clear my throat and mimic his deep, gravelly voice. "*You don't have proof that it was my daughter.*" I roll my eyes. "He was exceptionally rude. I mean, I guess it's cool how he had his daughter's back. Good for her. But he didn't have to be so condescending."

"Ah." Simone snaps her fingers like she figured out something. "He pressed your *daddy issues* button."

My eyes roll at the mention of my father. "Daddy issues or not, the guy was a jerk. And he insulted my costume."

Fatima shakes her head. "Hot guys can be such assholes."

I nudge Simone's shoulder with mine. "Except yours. I think you got the last one."

"He's not the last one." A sly smile creeps onto her face. "He is pretty amazing though, isn't he?"

I chuckle. "He is. So, let's go celebrate your marriage and forget about my neighbor."

For now.

2

GRANT

"Whatcha lookin' at?"

My shoulders jump, and I clutch at my chest. "Jesus, kid. I'm gonna make you wear a bell."

"I was literally just standing there." Noah rolls her eyes like the dramatic teen she is. "Can I see what you're looking at?"

"No." I tilt my phone away from her and zoom in so I can see better.

A woman with blonde hair skulks across my lawn, unaware of the Ring surveillance camera catching her every move. Then she crouches down near the edge of the porch.

What the fuck is she doing?

"That's the woman from across the street."

I place my phone face-down on the table. "Eat your breakfast before it gets cold."

Noah walks around the table and drops into the chair across from me. "I can eat and look at your phone at the same time, Dad."

I pinch the bridge of my nose and let out a long sigh. "If I let you look, will you stop fighting me on everything?"

"I don't fight you on everything."

I arch a brow. *Like right now?*

"I'm simply pointing out that I can do what you're telling me to do at the same time as doing what I want to do." She makes a show of biting off a piece of bacon. "I'd call that a compromise."

"Here." I slide the phone across the table. "I don't have the energy for your litigation today."

Noah snatches it and pulls it close to her face. "What the heck is she doing in our front yard in the middle of the night?"

"Maybe she's looking for the candy bowl you stole."

My phone slips out of her hands and clatters to the table as her eyes shoot to meet mine. "W-what?"

I rock onto the back legs of the chair and lock eyes with my daughter. "Did you take her bowl?"

"I...uh..." She swallows hard. "We wanted—"

"That's not what I asked."

"We just—"

"Yes or no?"

Noah's shoulders slump. "Yes."

"Why?"

"Reese wanted to—"

"Don't tell me about what Reese wanted." I let the chair fall onto four legs and lean my elbows onto the table. "Tell me why *you* would steal someone's property."

"I'm trying to explain, but you keep interrupting me."

"Because I don't want to hear an excuse, Noah. You're caught. Own up to it."

"Maybe I'll own up to it when you're ready to actually listen to me."

"Go ahead." I scoop a giant forkful of scrambled eggs into my mouth and mumble around it. "I'm listening."

Noah plays with the edge of her napkin. "It was Reese's idea to take the candy—not an excuse, just stating the facts. She was making fun of me to the other girls, saying that I wouldn't do it because I was too scared. She always calls me a goodie."

I hold up my hand to stop her. "I'm not interrupting, but I want to know what a goodie is."

"It's the opposite of a baddie."

"And what the hell is a baddie?"

"It's another word for a *badass*."

I fight the urge to roll my eyes. "Doing the wrong thing doesn't make you a badass."

"Well, I had to show her that I wasn't scared. I had to prove myself to her."

"You don't have to prove yourself to anyone, Noah. You—"

"You said you wouldn't interrupt!"

I stifle a groan. "Sorry."

"I was planning on returning the bowl. But then Reese tossed it into the street and it broke." She hikes a shoulder and I almost feel bad for her because she looks like the helpless little girl I used to know before the hormonal teenager took up residence in her body. "I've been trying to glue it back together all morning, but it won't hold."

My eyebrows jump. "You have the bowl?"

She nods, her messy brown hair falling in her eyes. "I felt bad for stealing it. That lady looked really upset."

Blonde Black Widow flashes through my mind. I haven't been able to shake her from my thoughts since she showed up on my porch dressed in head-to-toe spandex.

I rub the back of my neck. "She said it belonged to her grandmother."

"She *said*? Wait, how do you know about the bowl in the first place?"

"Because she told me."

Noah's mouth drops open.

"She stopped by to ask for her bowl back. She said she saw you and your friends running off with it."

"What did you say?"

I snap a strip of bacon in half and toss a piece into my mouth. "I told her she was wrong to come over to my house accusing *my* daughter of stealing something, because *my* daughter wouldn't do something like that. I told her *my* daughter has a strong backbone, and she wouldn't let her dumbass friends peer pressure her into doing something so stupid—not to mention illegal. I told her—"

"Okay, okay." She covers her face with her hands. "I get it. I'm a horrible person."

"You're not a horrible person. But you will be if you keep hanging out with people like Reese."

"What do you want me to do? The girls are, like, obsessed with her ever since she moved here. It's like she took over, and now everything we do is whatever Reese wants to do."

I drop my bacon onto the plate. "You need to talk to your friends. Tell them how you're feeling. I guarantee they're feeling the same way you do. And stand up to Reese. Don't let her push you around. You're an alpha. Don't let someone else boss you around or peer pressure you. Stand up to her."

The chair scrapes against the floor as Noah shoots out of it. "How many times do I have to tell you? I'm not an alpha. I'm not like you. I'll never be like you, Dad. Sorry to disappoint you." She stomps out of the kitchen and down the hall. "And by the way, you're not supposed to be eating bacon because of your high blood pressure."

The walls rattle with the slam of her door.

I scrub my face with both hands. *Well, that went well.*

Ever since Noah turned fourteen, it's like a switch went off somewhere in the universe. I'm speaking French while Noah is speaking Spanish, and neither one of us can understand the other.

I shove away my plate, unable to find my appetite.

I pick up my phone again and slide my finger along the bottom of the surveillance video, fast forwarding to the end where Blondie picks up something from my lawn and wraps it inside her coat before darting across the street to her house.

What was she doing down there?

I rewind it and zoom in as much as I can, but it's too dark, and the video is blurry.

I push out of my chair and head outside to see for myself. The hundred-pound pit bull we rescued last month follows me to the front door, but I tug his collar. "You stay inside, Romeo."

He whines and flops onto his belly in front of the door.

I pull up the video on my phone again and position myself in the same spot on my front lawn, facing my house. I scan the yard and step closer to the porch, retracing her steps.

And that's when I notice the bare space between two of my family of lawn gnomes.

Son of a bitch.

I glance over my shoulder and spot her white SUV across the street sitting in the driveway, so I march over to her house and ring the doorbell. After waiting several minutes, I ring it again.

She could be in the bathroom. Then again, the camera footage was time stamped well after two o'clock in the morning.

Aww, the princess is sleeping.

I push the doorbell rapid-fire fifty times until the door flies open.

"Jesus H. Christ. Who rings a doorbell like that?" Her sleepy eyes drag up to my face, and then she sucks in a gasp.

Her disheveled hair sticks up in every direction, half-hanging out of a messy bun. Black smudges surround her eyes, along with imprints of her bed sheet lining her cheeks. She's in nothing but an oversized tattered KISS T-shirt, and my gaze gets stuck a little too long on her thick thighs before I swing it back up to her crystal-blue eyes.

Get it together, man. Stop checking out the thief.

"Rough night?"

Her eyes narrow. "Come here to apologize?"

"No."

"Then what do you want?"

"I'm here for the gnome."

She scratches her head and looks around as if she doesn't know what I'm talking about. "Gnome?"

"You were on my lawn in the middle of the night, and you took it."

She tips her chin. "I don't know anything about this gnome you speak of."

"Maybe this will jog your memory." I face my phone to her and watch as her eyes widen for a split second when she sees herself crouching by my porch.

She hikes a nonchalant shoulder. "That's not me."

I almost laugh. "You know of another blonde who dressed up as Black Widow in our neighborhood last night?"

"That could've been anybody."

With those curves? No one in our neighborhood looks like her.

I slip my phone back into my pocket. "I could say the same for the person who ran off with your candy bowl. Could've been another brown-haired teen."

She balls her fists at her sides. "I saw your daughter in broad daylight—with my own two eyes, not some blurry camera. And why do you have a surveillance camera anyway? That's majorly creepy."

"Comes in handy when I need to catch a five-foot-nothing gnome thief."

She snorts. "I'm five two and a half."

"I'll be sure to tell the police that when I give them your description."

Her eyes roll. "Yes, because they'll send their whole search team over here just to look for a lawn ornament."

I clench my jaw, my patience wearing thin. "Just give up the damn gnome."

She pushes up onto her toes, yet she still doesn't come eye-to-eye with me. "Give me back my bowl."

I could go back to the house, ask Noah for the bowl, and put an end to this whole stupid thing. But there's something about this woman's self-righteous attitude that's tap-dancing on my last nerve.

I dip my head, closing the distance between us, bringing us nose to nose. "I don't have your damn bowl."

"Then I don't have your gnome."

We're at a stalemate, glaring at each other over inanimate objects.

"This is typical ignorant parent bullshit, you know." She shakes her head, and even though she's shorter, it feels like she's looking down her nose at me. "Everyone's all *not my* kid instead of talking to them about what they did wrong. It creates little brats who can't take accountability for their actions."

My patience snaps like a twig. "My daughter is not a brat."

"You're an enabler. You're not helping her in the long run."

"Do *you* have kids?"

She flinches like the words hit her in the face. "No. But I'm a teacher and—"

"Then you couldn't possibly understand what it feels like to have someone accuse your daughter of something. I don't care what you *say* she did—that's my kid, and I'll defend her until the day I die. I reprimand her how I see fit, and I raise her how I think she should be raised. And it's none of your goddamn business how I do it. So until you have kids of your own one day, stop tossing around insults at other people's kids."

Her eyes glisten and the angry façade falters.

Her voice shakes when she mutters a weak, "Fuck you."

Then she steps back and slams the door in my face.

What the hell just happened?

I'm two for two with women slamming doors on me today.

"Go away."

I rest my forehead on Noah's bedroom door. "Just open the door, please. I need to talk to you."

The door cracks open enough for Romeo to stick his nose into her room, his tail thumping against my leg.

"What?"

"I'm sorry I upset you earlier."

"Whatever."

"Not whatever. I'm trying to apologize here."

"You're always sorry, but you never change. What's the point of apologizing?"

Guilt stabs my heart. "Look, I know I suck at this whole dad thing, but I'm trying. I promise I'm trying."

Noah opens the door an inch wider. "You don't suck."

"We're two different people, so I'm trying to understand how you operate. But it's not easy. Everything is simple to me. If I'm mad, I tell someone why I'm mad. If I don't want to do something, I don't do it. I don't get these mean girl mind games." I hike a shoulder. "And I don't get why you'd steal someone's candy bowl just to prove yourself to some girl."

"She makes me so mad sometimes."

"What does Hannah think of Reese?"

She shrugs.

"Maybe you should talk to her. Hannah has been your best friend since you were in elementary school. Your friendship should be stronger than some new girl. Maybe Hannah feels the same way you do and is too afraid to talk to you about it."

"Maybe." Her eyes drop to her feet. "I'm trying to glue the bowl back together, but it's not working."

"Let me see."

She lets go of the doorknob, and Romeo pushes past me and leaps onto the bed.

It kills me every time I walk into Noah's room. Gone are the pink ruffles and little girl toys. *I want a room makeover,* she'd stated over dinner one night. *Everything is so babyish.* I offered to get her a new comforter, but she wanted more than that. So I painted the walls a seafoam-green color and gave her the shore-themed room she wanted. Lately, it feels like something changes every time I turn around, and the baby girl I once knew is slipping away piece by piece.

Having a teenager in the house sometimes feels like living with a stranger.

I lower myself onto the corner of her bed and examine the crime scene on the floor. "You're using the wrong kind of glue."

"Oh." Her head hangs. "All I have is Elmer's."

"I have Gorilla Glue in the garage. That'll do the trick." I flick my eyes to hers. "What happens after you put the bowl back together?"

She stares at the ceramic pieces. "I was going to leave it on her porch with a note."

"Hmm." I nod. "I'd like it if you rang her bell and talked to her, face to face."

She gasps as if I told her to run around the block without any clothes on. "Dad, no."

"Okay, okay."

Her eyebrows pull together. "Okay?"

"Yeah, okay."

"Why aren't you fighting me on it?"

"What do you want me to say?"

"Something like, '*If you did the crime, you need to own up to it. Stand there and look her in the eye and tell her what you did.*'" She shrugs. "Something like that."

My lip curls. "Why do I sound like a stuffy old British man?"

A laugh breaks free. "I don't know."

Warmth pools in my chest. "Been a while since I've heard the pretty sound of your laughter."

"Dad, stop." She fidgets with the hem of her shirt and glances around the room at nothing in particular.

Compliments make her feel awkward, so I'm not allowed to give them to her.

But I sneak one in every now and again because she deserves it.

"I want you to know that I hear you. You said you want to leave her a note, then you can leave her a note. What I would do in this situation is irrelevant." I grip her shoulder and give her a squeeze. "I think it was kind of you to save her bowl and try to fix it—even if the initial deed was unkind. I'm proud of you for that."

"Do you think she'll be mad about her bowl being broken?"

Lord only knows what the crazy woman across the street will think of this.

"I'm sure she'll be disappointed. But the bowl seems important to her, so she'll probably just be happy to have it back."

Noah lowers herself beside me. "Was that her on the Ring video you were watching this morning?"

I slip my phone out of my back pocket and tap on the app to pull up last night's footage. Romeo lifts his head as if he wants to watch too.

Noah leans in and her eyes narrow. "What was she doing?"

I grunt. "She stole the gnome off our lawn."

Her chin jerks back. "What?"

"Mr. Bubbles is officially in a hostage situation."

"Why would she…" Her eyes pop open wide. "It's because I stole her bowl. An eye for an eye."

"Looks that way."

She clamps her hand over her mouth as her shoulders shake. "That's pretty funny."

Funny? She is insufferable. "What grown adult steals someone's lawn ornament? It's immature behavior."

"She does look younger than you."

"Watch it, kid."

"I'm just saying. How old do you think she is?"

"Late twenties, maybe?" I rub my temples in small circles. "We should give back the bowl. Then she'll give back Mr. Bubbles."

Noah chews on her bottom lip. "We should. It's the right thing to do."

I shoot her a dubious look. "Sounds like there's a *but* coming."

"But…if Mr. Bubbles is being held hostage, then we need to fire back. W.W.B.D."

What Would Bruce Do.

My eyebrows hit my hairline. "I can't believe you still remember that."

"Of course I remember. We've seen every Bruce Willis movie known to man. He practically raised me."

I should tell her no. I shouldn't entertain whatever hair-brained plan she's going to concoct. But for the first time in a long time, we're having a conversation. She's talking. To me. And not in a shrill tone accusing me of not *understanding* her.

Plus, she brought Bruce into this.

I selfishly indulge, hoping it'll keep the smile on her face a little longer. "All right. What are you thinking?"

She rubs her palms together. "Leave it to me."

3

ELENA

"Hi, Miss Lenny."

I push my sunglasses to the top of my head. "Hi, Jake. How was school today?"

"It was awesome for a Monday."

"Oh, yeah?" I reach into my back seat and pull out my bags. "What happened to make it so awesome?"

"We auditioned for speaking parts in the Thanksgiving play and I got a part."

Val stifles a laugh. "Tell Miss Lenny which part you got."

"The turkey!"

My mouth drops open. "Dude. That's like, the leading role."

"I know." His blue eyes widen. "I have so many lines to practice. And I have to make my costume."

I adjust the purse strap on my shoulder. "I'm so proud of you. You're going to be the best turkey that school has ever seen."

"Will you come and watch me?"

My heart melts a little. "Of course. You just tell me the day and time, and I'll be there."

"It's November twentieth." A frown pulls at the corners of his mouth. "But it's during school. You'll be working."

I wave a dismissive hand. "That's the great thing about being an adult. If I need some time off from work, I don't have to go in."

"Really?" He hikes his shoulders. "That's pretty cool."

"The coolest."

Val holds out her hand. "Come on, Jake. Let the crazy bag lady get her things inside."

Jake eyes my totes. "You do carry a lot of bags."

"All teachers do." I shoot him a wink. "It's where we keep our magic."

He tries to wink back, but both of his eyes blink at the same time.

Val shakes her head. "We're working on that."

I chuckle. "Don't. It's cuter that way."

I lug my bags over to the mailbox and glance at the asshole's house across the street. I haven't seen him since our encounter on my porch Saturday morning. Embarrassment creeps into my cheeks as I think about the way I must have looked when I opened the door after waking up from my late night out—especially when he looked so sexy in his jeans and flannel.

His hotness only makes him more irritating.

The comment he made about me not having kids was the icing on the cake. I was two seconds away from letting him see me cry—which might have worked in my favor, but I have too much pride for that. Plus, it's not like he knows that I can't have children of my own. People with kids toss around that comment all the time. *You don't understand unless you have kids.* I get it. Maybe I don't know what it's like to raise a child, but saying that twists the knife in a perpetually open wound.

I flip open the mailbox and stick my hand inside, still glaring at his house over my shoulder.

But my fingers graze something furry, and my hand jerks back. Bending down, I peer inside.

Then a scream tears from my chest.

Halfway to her house, Val spins around. "Lenny, what's wrong?"

"It's in my mailbox." I back away and point. "There's a tarantula in my mailbox."

"Cool!" Jake runs toward me. "Can I see?"

"Don't touch it, Jake." Val trails behind him. "We're in Jersey. How the hell did a tarantula get in your mailbox?"

Jake scrunches his face and looks at his mother like she's a fool. "Lots of different kinds of spiders live in New Jersey."

I drop my bags on the sidewalk and run my fingernails over my arms. "Oh god. I'm getting itchy. What if she laid eggs in there? I'll have to move. Where's a place that doesn't have tarantulas, Jake?"

"It's probably not a tarantula. The wolf spider lives here, and it's furry like a tarantula. It's an easy mistake to make."

"Stop scratching. You're making me itchy." Val nudges me with her elbow. "Don't get too close, Jake. I know you're curious, but you don't know what this thing might do to you."

"It won't bite me." Jake sighs like he's irritated that he has to explain this. "It's not an aggressive kind of spider, and it doesn't like people."

"The feeling is mutual." I groan. "How am I going to get it out of there?"

Jake peers inside the mailbox, squinting to see. "Wow. That's pretty big."

Val lowers her voice. "This is one of those times you don't want to hear a sentence like that."

I clamp my hand over my mouth to keep from laughing. "This is not the time for dick jokes."

"Wait a second." Jake reaches into the mailbox.

Val screeches. "Stop, don't touch it!"

But the little shit lifts the spider out by its leg and flings it at us.

Val shields her head with her hands and drops to the ground, and I take off, clawing out of my jacket and tossing it behind me—both of us screaming like lunatics.

"It's not real, you guys." Jake plants his hands on his knees, hunched over as he laughs. "It's a fake spider."

"A fake spider?" I slow down and make my way back to my mailbox. "Are you sure?"

"See for yourself." He kicks it over with his shoe, revealing a barcode sticker stuck to the spider's underbelly.

Val slaps her palm against her chest. "Jesus Christ, Jake. Are you trying to kill your mother?"

He grins and reaches out his hand to help her up. "Miss Lenny, who put a fake spider in your mailbox?"

My eyes flick to the house across the street, and the curtain covering one of the windows sways back and forth.

I grit my teeth, anger swelling inside my chest like a wave. "Oh, I think I might have an idea."

Val arches a brow as she follows my line of sight. "You don't think it was Grant Harper's daughter, do you?"

Grant Harper. "Tall, dark, and doesn't talk to anyone?"

"Yes, and his daughter is Noah." She covers Jake's ears. "I heard from Lucy's daughter down the block that she's been hanging out with the wrong crowd at school. Poor thing doesn't have a mother. What do you expect?"

"I don't think it was Noah who put the tarantula in my mailbox. I think it was her father."

"No way." Val waves a dismissive hand. "Why would he do something like that to you?"

"Have you ever spoken to him?"

"No. He doesn't speak to anyone in the neighborhood."

"I had the lovely pleasure of talking with him on Friday."

Jake removes Val's hands from his ears. "She doesn't mean it was a lovely pleasure. She's being sarcastic, Mom."

"Yeah, I got that, kid." Val leans in. "What happened?"

I tell Val—and inadvertently Jake—about the candy bowl fiasco, and our conversation thereafter.

"See?" She points her index finger at me. "I told you: His daughter is a little criminal in the making."

"Well, don't tell her father that or he'll bite your head off."

Jake's eyebrows pull together in a pensive expression. "So, she stole your bowl; you stole his gnome; and he put a fake spider in your mailbox. It's your turn to retaliate."

Val clicks her tongue on the roof of her mouth. "Jake, that's not nice. We don't retaliate. We have to be the bigger people and talk about them behind their backs like normal civilized humans."

"There are no rules in a prank war, Mom."

I laugh. "I've never been in the midst of a prank war. I guess I can Google some ideas."

"I'm pretty good with pranks."

Val nods in agreement with her son. "It's true. He got me with the old tape-on-the-sink-hose prank."

"But I can't get into his house. It has to be something outside." I kneel down in front of the little prankster. "You have any ideas?"

It's immature and petty, resorting to advice from a child. But Jake is right: It's my turn to retaliate.

And after the spider in my mailbox, Grant just declared war.

"Are you serious?"

"Of course I'm serious, Simone." I sandwich the phone between my ear and my shoulder and yank out the cork from the wine bottle. "Guys like this expect everyone to back down. I've gotta show him that I'm not afraid."

"Unless there's a fake spider in your mailbox."

"It looked real. You would've screamed too."

"Good thing the six-year-old next door was there to save you."

I tip the bottle over my glass and hold it there, dumping a copious amount of wine into the glass. "Jake is the best kid ever. He has so many good prank ideas."

"So, how is pranking the hot guy across the street going to get your candy bowl back?"

"It's not." I lift the glass to my lips and take a long sip. "It's not about the bowl anymore. It's about showing him that I won't stand to be treated like this."

"By stooping to his level."

"I'm fighting back." A slow smile stretches across my lips as I imagine the look on his face when he gets a taste of his own medicine. "Maybe I should install a Ring camera of my own so I can catch it in case I'm not home to see it."

"You'd better be careful. He's the one with all the footage of you on his property in the middle of the night. I don't have bail money."

"Pfft. You can't see my face on the video."

"Not my point." Simone pauses. "Why are you getting so bent out of shape about this guy? It's not like you to act like this."

I gulp down more wine and slump down into my favorite chair in the living room. "I don't know. He's...irritating. He probably bullies everyone in his life, and they're too afraid to stand up to him."

"Does it have anything to do with the fact that you're scorned by your ex-husband and your father, so you're on the attack with all men?"

A frown tugs at the corners of my mouth. "No."

Maybe.

"If you want my expert opinion, it sounds like you're trying to get back at your neighbor because you can't get back at Neil."

My stomach roils at the sound of my ex-husband's name. "Look, I know I'm quick to get defensive with men ever since I caught Neil with another woman. But Grant—whom we shall not refer to as *hot neighbor* anymore—was totally rude to me. If he apologized about the bowl, then things would've gone a lot differently. I can't let him think he can treat me like that."

"I love that you want to stick up for yourself. But I don't think this is the way to do it. I think your wounds are still fresh after hearing about Neil getting his whore pregnant and you're looking for someone to take out your anger on."

I spin the glass stem between my fingers as I ponder Simone's point. "I don't think she's a whore. I think she fell in love."

"Yeah, with someone else's husband."

"I couldn't give him a child, and now he's having one. It's for the best." Unexpected tears spring into my eyes. "I just want the pain to stop. But there it is, every time I look into Jake's eyes or when one of my students hugs me. Even when Grant's daughter took off with my bowl, for a split second, I thought about how I would handle it if she were my daughter."

"Oh, honey. I wish I could say the right thing to make you feel better, but I know nothing will."

I swipe a tear from my cheek. "It's okay."

"One thing I can tell you is this: Don't let losers like your father and Neil taint your view on men. You'll find someone who treats you the way you deserve to be treated."

"I sure hope so." I sniffle. "Until then, I'll focus on serving justice to the asshole across the street."

"All right. Tell me your plan so I can help you not get arrested."

4

GRANT

"You all right, old man?"

I scoff. "I'm six months older than you. If I'm an old man, so are you."

Trent points to my legs. "But I'm not walking like I'm eighty."

"My back has been killing me this week. I'm injured, not old."

"You should go to my chiropractor. She'll twist you like a pretzel." Mitch waggles his wiry gray eyebrows. "She's got strong hands. I love a woman with strong hands."

Jason shakes his head. "The only way you can get a woman to put her hands on you is by giving her a copay."

"Fuck off. I got more women in my day than you've had in your whole life."

"Highly doubtful."

"Would you two quit it? I refuse to go to happy hour with you bickering like a married couple." Trent tosses his hard hat into the back seat of his car. "Grant, please come and save me from these two."

"Not tonight."

Jason stops beside my truck. "Ah, come on. Have a beer with us and watch the game."

"I can't. I have to get home for Noah."

"She's fourteen. She can handle herself for a little while." Trent chuckles. "Hell, we were always on our own when we were fourteen."

"That's the point. I don't want her to grow up the way we did." I swing open my passenger door and sit my tool bag on the floor inside. "She's been hanging out with this new girl who's causing trouble and I need to keep an eye on her."

Trent leans against the truck. "Noah's a good kid though. She won't go along with peer pressure."

"She stole a neighbor's candy bowl on Halloween. Took off with the bowl and everything. The neighbor caught her and came and told me."

"We all did stupid shit when we were younger." Mitch shoves his hands in his pockets. "It's okay if she gets into a little trouble here and there. As long as you give her consequences for her actions."

"She said she feels like she has to prove herself to this new girl." I shake my head. "I'm out of my league here. I don't know how to change that."

"You can't change it. She's gotta figure it out for herself." Trent shrugs. "That's how we all learned. You can't put her in a bubble."

I understand what they're saying, but logic doesn't mean shit when it comes to my daughter. "I want her to do the right thing and stay out of trouble."

"I'm just saying you're allowed to go out and have a little fun every once in a while." Trent rests a hand on my shoulder. "I'm worried about you."

"What is this, an intervention?"

Mitch arches a brow. "Do you need one?"

"Fuck no."

Trent lets out a long sigh. "I know you went through a lot with Tara but—"

"No. This has nothing to do with Tara."

Jason looks between us. "Who's Tara?"

"Noah's mother." Her name strikes a nerve in me like it always does. "How does me not going out for a beer have anything to do with Tara?"

"She went down a bad path and you couldn't stop her. Now you see Noah making bad decisions and you're scared she'll end up the same way as her mother." Trent jabs my chest with his index finger. "But you can't control her any more than you could've controlled Tara."

I clench my jaw. "Noah will not end up the same way her mother did."

"You can't sit home all day to make sure of that. Look at you. You're barely living. You go to work, come home, and do it all again the next day."

"And you're grouchy as fuck," Jason adds.

"How long have you been single now?" Mitch asks. "Noah's a teenager."

"She's fourteen, but that's not the—"

"You haven't fucked anyone in fourteen *years*?" Jason's eyes widen. "Shit. You *do* need an intervention."

I roll my eyes. "Just because I'm single doesn't mean I haven't had sex, dipshit."

I just won't tell him how few and far between the sex has been.

Trent levels me with a look. "Aren't you tired of being alone? How are you going to meet anyone if you won't even make time for your friends, let alone go on a date?"

"I'm alone because I choose to be alone. Raising that kid is my number one priority. Everything else takes a back seat."

"Until when?" Trent tilts his head. "Your life is practically half over."

Jason grunts. "And your dick's lifespan is more than half over too."

"I have Noah, and that's all I need." I swing open my door and get into the driver's seat. "Leave my dick out of this."

I PULL into my driveway and put the truck in park.

Before I head inside, I glance at the house across the street in my rear-view mirror and fight the smirk tugging at my lips for the third time today. I can still hear Blondie's high-pitched scream after she touched the fake spider in her mailbox. It was even funnier when she tore off her jacket as she flailed down the block after the kid tossed the spider at her. I should drop by his house and leave him some of my leftover Halloween candy as a thank you.

As much as I hate to admit it, Noah did good with that idea. I shouldn't stoke the flames of her troublemaking side, but it was a harmless prank, and it felt good to knock my neighbor off her high horse.

Should I be messing with my neighbor? No.

Should I condone this behavior with Noah watching? Definitely not.

But nothing irritates me more than when people impose parenting advice on others. With Noah's mom out of the picture, everyone thinks they have the right to tell me how to raise my daughter.

Getting back at Blondie makes me feel better in a fucked-up way.

I exit the truck and stagger up the porch steps, trying to not put any weight on my right leg.

Add sciatica to my I'm-getting-old list.

A small cardboard box sits beside my door—without a label or address.

I grunt as I bend down to pick it up, pins and needles stabbing my leg. I examine the box as I wrap my other hand around the knob on the screen door. But when I pull it open, my hand slips off and I fly backward. I try to catch myself but then I teeter over the top step and end up sprawled out on my front lawn like a starfish, staring up at the sky.

Noah bursts through the door with Romeo on her heels. "Dad, are you okay?"

A pained groan escapes me. "I'm just fucking peachy."

"What happened?" She runs down the stairs and holds out her hand for me.

Romeo dive bombs me, licking my face like he hasn't seen me in months. "Get off me. Your breath stinks."

Noah pulls me to a seated position and plucks the box from the grass. "Who's this from?"

"Open it."

She tears open the top flap and gasps. "It's Mr. Bubbles."

My teeth gnash together and I glare down at my Vaseline-covered palm.

Well played, Blondie. Well fucking played.

Noah's eyebrows press together. "Why would she give him back if we didn't return her bowl?"

"It was a diversion." I push off the ground, ignoring the shooting pain in my back, and jerk my head. "Come on. And get your dog inside before he spots a squirrel."

Inside, I head to the kitchen and snatch the dish towel off the oven handle, wiping off the residue from my hand. "Did the doorbell ring while you were home?"

Noah shakes her head as she digs into the freezer for my ice pack. "I took a shower when I got home. Why?"

I slip out my phone and pull up the Ring camera footage, scrolling to three-thirty. "Here she is."

Blondie's face fills the screen at three-thirty-four. She's holding the box up to block her right hand. To anyone else, she looks like she's ringing the doorbell to deliver a package. But I know what she's really doing.

Noah leans in. "She rang the bell?"

"Nope. She greased the doorknob and left."

Noah's hand clamps over her mouth and her eyes widen.

Yeah, she's good. I was so fixated on the box that I didn't notice the globs of Vaseline on the doorknob.

I take the ice pack from Noah and shove it under the back of my shirt as I ease down onto the kitchen chair.

"You okay?"

I give her a tight nod. "I'll be fine."

"You should go to the doctor about your back."

"It's fine."

"Dad—"

"Got another prank idea?"

She crosses her arms over her chest, looking a hell of a lot like me when I'm pissed. "Don't change the subject."

"It's just sciatica. It's fine."

"But you're in pain. They could give you pain medication."

"I'm not taking pain meds."

"What about an injection? My friend Charlotte's father got an injection in his spine to help with the pain from his accident."

"I wasn't in an accident. And I don't want a needle in my spine."

Her nose wrinkles. "You're the biggest baby."

"You hungry? I'll order a pizza."

Romeo's ears perk up at the mention of food.

Noah lets out a frustrated sigh and turns to walk away. "Whatever."

"Hey." I tug her hand before she can leave. "You don't have to worry about me. It's normal for construction workers to be in pain and—"

"Is it because of Mom?"

The question stops me in my tracks. "What?"

"Are you scared of taking pills because of Mom?"

She hasn't asked about her mother in a couple of years. It's probably because I avoid this topic whenever she brings it up.

"I take Tylenol if the pain gets bad, but I don't need anything else. I'll be fine."

Noah nods and chews her bottom lip, quiet as she mulls over whatever's going on in her mind.

I should ask her what she's thinking. I should say more.

Instead, I pull up the pizzeria in my contacts and lift the phone to my ear. "I'll get half with mushrooms and peppers for you."

I know I can't evade her questions forever, but it's complicated and I don't know how to talk about this with her.

One day I'll tell her everything.

But not today.

5

LENNY

I STIFLE a yawn as I swing myself into my car.

Apple Car Play connects when I turn on the engine and Breaking Benjamin comes through the speakers. My head falls back against the headrest and I take a sip of coffee, letting the music soothe my soul.

Most people hate waking up for work in the morning, but I love it. The world is quiet and dark, the sun barely kissing the horizon. It's calm, with promise of the day ahead.

It helps that I love my job too. As much as school administrators try to crush our spirit, we're renewed when we see our students' smiling faces each day. It's amazing to be responsible for so much—their learning, the molding of who they are as humans, and who they'll become. We make a difference, whether we realize it or not. Contrary to the rude dickhead across the street, teachers are with students more often than their parents are—so I know a thing or two about the importance of being a role model for them.

I shift my car into reverse and glance at my backup camera.

And a terrifying bloody face fills the screen.

Fear seizes me and I let out a yelp as I slam on my brakes.

What the fuck?

I throw the car into park, swing open my door, and stomp

around to the rear of the vehicle. Sure enough, the terrifying image is taped to my backup camera.

I tear it off and crumble it in my hand, shooting a dirty look at the house across the street.

"Asshole."

I get back in the car and continue on my way to work.

This is getting ridiculous now. I could end it all by ignoring this prank. But taking the high road feels a lot like giving in.

And there isn't a reality in which I'd let Grant win.

I'm going to need some more ideas.

I SPEND every day Googling pranks for the next week.

It's probably eating at Grant not knowing if and when I'll retaliate, which makes the wait even sweeter.

And right now, the wait was so worth it.

"Okay, are you sure you remember your lines?"

Val nods. "Yes, I'm positive. I've been practicing for two days straight."

"And you're sure you don't mind getting roped into my drama?"

"I live for drama, baby." Val pats the box and shoots me a wink. "This is the highlight of my year."

"You need to get out more."

"I really do." She slips her phone into the breast pocket on her jacket. "Does this look obvious?"

"Not at all." I adjust it so the camera isn't obscured. "It just looks like you have your phone sticking out of your pocket."

She salutes me. "Wish me luck."

"Break a leg."

As soon as Val closes the door behind her, I run upstairs and dive onto my bed, peeking through the blinds covering my window. My heart races in suspense as I watch her make her way over to Grant's house and ring his bell.

It's too far away for me to make out his expression, but a laugh rips from my chest when I see his hands shoot up on either side of his head. He refuses to take the box from Val as she thrusts it toward him.

It's a dildo—the biggest I could find—in a conspicuous box addressed to him.

Not many friends will pretend that the mailman delivered a dildo to her that was addressed to him, creating a fake label and all. I feel sad for anyone who doesn't have a Val in their lives.

After a few minutes, Val jogs back across the street, but she heads home instead of coming to my house so Grant doesn't know it was me. He keeps his eyes on her until she disappears inside her house, and I wait on bated breath for her text.

My phone vibrates, and I press play on Val's video.

Grant opens his door with his signature scowl in place. "Can I help you?"

Val holds out the box with a picture of a massive-sized hot pink dildo on the front. "This was delivered to me by accident."

Grant's eyes pop out of his head as his hands go up. "That isn't mine."

"Well, it's addressed to you." Val taps on the shipping label we printed out. "Grant Harper. That's you, right?"

"No. I mean, yes, that's me. But *that* isn't mine."

"Please, you don't have to be embarrassed. Everyone uses these things nowadays."

"I don't." He takes a step back, his eyes darting from the box to Val. "I didn't order that."

"Hmm. Maybe your daughter ordered it?"

Grant chokes on his spit and his face turns ten shades of red. "Nobody in this house ordered a…a…"

"Dildo." Val raises her voice. "It's called a dildo."

He steps out onto the porch and closes his door behind him. "Lower your voice. I don't want my daughter to hear you."

"You know, masturbation is a totally normal thing for teenagers her age. Maybe she's curious and—"

Grant snatches the box out of Val's hand. "Get off my property. Now."

Val doesn't miss a beat. "Your secret's safe with me, Grant."

I clutch my stomach as I laugh and press Val's name on my screen to call her.

"Hello, is this the academy calling?" she answers.

I laugh harder. "That was perfect. You were amazing. I didn't even think to blame it on his daughter."

"I'm great at ad libbing."

"You missed your calling for sure."

"He tossed it in his garbage can before he went back inside. I didn't catch that part on camera though."

"I'm going to save this video for the rest of my life. And watch it often."

"His face got really red. I was almost concerned about his blood pressure."

"Thank you so much for doing this. Seriously, Val. You're a good friend."

"I've got your back, kid." She heaves a sigh. "I do worry about how far he'll take this though. Like at what point does this end?"

The smile falls from my face as I sober. "I don't know."

How far am I willing to take this?

My thoughts are interrupted by a text, followed by a string of them.

Neil: I called you yesterday.
Neil: Are you busy?
Neil: Can we talk?
Neil: Answer me.

I groan. "Neil is texting me. Let me go deal with this."

Val gasps. "He's still bothering you about the house?"

"Yup."

"The things I would do to hurt that man if I knew I wouldn't get caught…"

"I draw the line at letting you deliver dildos."

"This isn't funny, Len. He cheated on you and got his side piece pregnant, yet he's still hounding you to sell the house? He shouldn't be doing this."

"I'm hoping he'll be preoccupied once the baby is born, and he'll forget about me."

"And if he doesn't? What are you going to do?"

"I don't know." I glance around my bedroom. "Maybe it's bad juju keeping this house. Maybe I should sell it and start over."

"Don't you dare give in to that asshole's demands. You will die in that house and even then, I will make sure your body stays rotting in there for a good long while before calling it in, just to spite him."

I choke out a laugh. "You've thought about this, I see."

"I'd get it if you said you didn't want to live there because it was your shared home. But you love that house and I don't want you to sell it because he bullied you into it. Sell it if you want to sell it."

She's right. I do love this house, despite the fact that I bought it with a man who broke my heart.

"Maybe I can change my number."

"He still knows where you live. I don't put it past him to show up unannounced like a stalker."

My stomach twists at the thought.

"You should get The Ring camera. This way, if he shows up at your house, you can use the footage as proof in court."

Again with the creepy camera?

"Those aren't for me."

"It's better to have it than not. Promise me you'll think about it."

"Fine. I'll think about it."

"Good. All right, let me go. I have a kid to bathe and a dinner to prep." She sucks her teeth. "I'm a famous actress now. I shouldn't have to deal with this shit."

I laugh and tell her goodnight. But before I put my phone down, I tap out a text to Neil.

Me: Just because I agreed to split the money with you if I sell the house doesn't give you the right to bully me into selling it. Please leave me alone.

Neil: I'm not bullying you. Stop being so dramatic.

Neil: I just want to talk. It's a buyer's market now. You could get a nicer house if you sell the one you're in.

Me: I don't want a nicer house. I like this one.

Me: Focus on getting your house ready for the baby and stop texting me.

Neil: Don't throw my child in my face like that.

Me: Lose my number and I won't have to.

Then I click through my settings and block Neil's number.

6

ELENA

After school the next day, I pick up some dry-cleaning and head home.

When I turn down my block, I spot Grant's daughter running along the sidewalk.

My top lip curls. *On the run after stealing another candy bowl?*

Then I get closer and see the expression on her face.

Eyes wide, head frantic as she whips it back and forth like she's searching for something. Tears stream down her rosy cheeks. She cups her hands around her mouth and shouts, loud enough for me to hear her strangled cry from inside my car.

Worry clenches around my stomach.

Where's her father?

I jerk the steering wheel to the left and hop out as soon as I throw my car into park. "Hey, what's wrong?"

The girl wipes her dripping nose on the back of her sleeve. "My dog…he ran out of the house…he saw a squirrel."

They have the cutest pit bull. I've seen him the many times my nose was plastered against my window while I watched Grant jog around the neighborhood with him last spring.

I'm not proud of that fact.

I wave her toward my car. "Get in. We'll cover more ground if we drive."

She freezes. "Seriously? You're going to help me?"

I could drive home and tell the kid she's on her own. But I've seen the way people whip around the corners in this neighborhood, and I couldn't live with myself if something happened to the dog.

"I'm a dog person." I jerk my head. "Let's go."

She jumps into my passenger seat, and I roll down both windows.

"What's your dog's name?"

"Romeo." A tear slips down her cheek. "He's such a sweetheart."

"Pit bulls usually are. And what's your name?"

"Noah." She leans out the window making kissy noises with her lips. "Romeo! Here, boy!"

We take turns calling his name as I circle the block.

"Does he have a favorite spot on the walks you go on?"

She shakes her head. "He likes the dog park, but we drive there. It'd be too far for him to get to and he wouldn't know where to go. Oh, God. What if something happens to him?"

I place my hand on her knee. "We'll find him. Don't worry."

"My dad's going to kill me." She covers her face with her hands and sobs shake her shoulders. "He's going to say how irresponsible I am. He always tells me to make sure I close the screen door and listen for the click because it doesn't fully close."

"Look, people make mistakes and accidents happen. Don't focus on what your father is going to say, and focus on getting your dog back."

I rack my brain, trying to think of anything that might help us find Noah's dog. "What about a favorite toy…does he have one?"

She nods. "It's a cloth duck with a squeaker inside of it."

"Doesn't he rip it to shreds?"

She shakes her head and her brown hair falls in her face. "My dad sews it if he makes a hole."

I cough out a laugh. "Your dad knows how to sew?"

"He knows how to do everything."

Well, he certainly is an expert at being a dick.

But I bite my tongue, not about to talk shit in front of the asshole's kid. It's not her fault her dad sucks. "Let's go back to your house and grab the squeaker. Maybe he'll hear it and come running."

Noah's eyes widen with hope. "That might work."

"I have some leftover steak in my fridge. I'll bring that too. Does he respond to the word *treat*?"

She nods. "He loves treats."

My brakes screech to a stop in front of her house and we both run in opposite directions to grab our supplies. "Grab his leash while you're in there," I call over my shoulder.

Two minutes later, we're back in the car on the hunt.

Noah squeaks the toy out the window as I roll by slowly. "Romeo. Come on, boy. Where are you?"

A flash of black and white darts out from behind someone's fence, ears standing at attention when he hears the toy.

"There he is!" Noah flings open the door and hops out of the car before I can fully stop.

"Jesus Christ, kid." I pull over and run after her, waving the steak in my hands. "Don't chase him, Noah. He'll think it's a game."

She freezes. "What do we do?"

"Sit down criss cross-applesauce." I lower myself onto the sidewalk and toss a piece of steak at Romeo. "Want some steak? Yeah, you do. Come and get it. Come on, boy."

Romeo darts over to the steak bite and gobbles it up.

I lower my voice as if he can understand me. "Noah, I'm going to lure him over here and then you grab his collar."

She nods and pushes to her knees, at the ready.

I outstretch my arm and lean forward. "Want more?"

Romeo looks between us like he's unsure if he trusts us. But his desire for food outweighs his doubt and he trots over to eat from my hand.

"Good boy." I stroke his head while Noah clips his leash on him.

She throws her arms around his neck. "Romeo, you crazy dog.

You scared me half to death." With tears glistening in her dark eyes, she looks up at me. "Thank you so much."

I give her a nod. "Come on. Let's get you guys home."

Romeo bounds into the back seat with his tongue lolling out of the side of his mouth.

Noah scoots into the back with him. "I'm sorry about the dog hair in advance. He sheds like crazy."

"It's fine. Nobody ever sits back there."

When we pull onto our street, Noah lets out a long groan at the same time I spot her father in front of his house. He's wearing a worried expression on his face, much like the one his daughter wore not twenty minutes ago when she couldn't find her dog.

"Everything is okay. We have Romeo, and you're both safe."

She scoffs. "You don't know my father."

I laugh. "Oh, I've had the pleasure of meeting him."

Noah's cheeks burn and her eyes drop to her lap.

I pull into Grant's driveway and blow out a breath between my lips, attempting to calm my nervous belly.

Show time.

Noah opens her door first and Romeo leaps out and jumps up with his paws on his chest.

Grant staggers backward and glares at me through my window as he rips open my door. "What the fuck are you doing with my daughter?"

I slide out of the seat. "I was—"

"Why. The fuck. Are you with. My daughter?"

I gesture to the dog. "I was—"

"You want to play your little pranks on me, go ahead. But you don't come near my daughter, do you understand me?" He stabs the air with his finger. "Stay away from her."

I plant my hands on my hips. "I was helping her. You would know that if you'd let me finish my goddamn sentence."

He grits his teeth. "No more games. Just leave us alone."

"Dad, stop." Noah steps between us. "This is my fault. I lost Romeo. He ran out of the house and I couldn't find him, and she pulled over to help." She turns to me and wraps her arms around my waist.

I falter back a few steps, not expecting the hug.

"I was so rude to you and you helped me anyway." She sniffles. "Thank you so much."

I meet Grant's eyes as I place my palm on the back of his daughter's head, holding her in my embrace. "I was happy to help. I'm glad we found Romeo."

Grant watches us with his unwavering stony expression. His chest heaves as he sucks in breath after breath, looking like he's about to blow a gasket.

Noah's shoulders shake as she cries. "I'm so sorry I stole your candy bowl. I have it still, you know. I glued it back together. When you stole Mr. Bubbles, I thought it would be fun to prank you back. But it must suck for you because you didn't ask for any of this. I'm sorry." Her head jerks back as she looks up at me. "I don't even know your name."

I smile. "It's Lenny."

She buries her head in my coat again. "I'm sorry, Lenny."

"It's okay. Your dad and I are the grown-ups here. We could've both handled this much better." I glare at him when I toss out the word both. "You remember what I said in the car? People make mistakes. Keep my bowl as a reminder of that." I pry myself from her grip and hold her out in front of me. "Let's call this a truce, okay?"

"Yes. Definitely." She nods before glancing at her father. "Right, Dad? Truce."

His jaw muscles pop. "Get the dog inside, Noah. And leave your iPad on the kitchen table. You're grounded."

Both of our mouths fall open.

"What? Seriously, Dad? Grounded for what?"

"I've told you time and time again to make sure the screen door locks. Yes, people make mistakes, but they also have to learn from them. Otherwise, they keep making the same mistakes."

I step forward. "With all due respect, sir, I don't think it's necessary to ground her. It was—"

"I don't need parenting advice from someone who isn't a parent."

He spits it with such venom, it pierces my chest like an arrow.

Tears sting the backs of my eyes, but I don't back down this time. "You're right: People need consequences to learn from their mistakes, but kids are going to mess up a little more frequently than adults. I might not be a parent, but that doesn't mean I don't know about children. I have a master's degree in this area, which is a lot more knowledge than some parents are concerned. Maybe you should take a look at yourself instead of pointing the finger at me."

He opens his mouth to speak but I hold up my hand in his face. "Do not cut me off again. It's rude and dismissive, and if I have to listen to your condescending words, then you can listen to mine."

His mouth clamps shut.

"I came to your house last week to inform you that my bowl was stolen. You turned a blind eye to your daughter's indiscretion and yelled at me instead. That's not what a good parent does. And fuck you for that, by the way, sir, because you sure aren't winning any parent of the year awards. Your daughter was scared shitless for accidentally letting the dog loose. Maybe you should fix the lock on the door instead of yelling at her when the dog gets out. Better yet, you should train your dog not to run out of the house. You want to be a jackass to me, then have at it. But do *not* take this out on your daughter. You didn't ground her when she stole my property, yet you're grounding her for the dog getting out? You're just mad she was with me, so you're punishing her for it."

I let my eyes roam over Grant's body. "You know, I used to think you were this strong, attractive, amazing dad, but it turns out: You're nothing but a typical, insecure, rude man who's clearly over-compensating for something in his life."

Before he can utter another word, I spin around and get into my car without another glance in his direction.

7

GRANT

Noah hasn't spoken a word to me since Blondie peeled out of our driveway yesterday.

I punished her, so she's punishing me with silence.

I tap my fork against Noah's dish. "How long will you be giving me the silent treatment for?"

She pretends like she doesn't hear me.

I push back my plate and lean against my chair. "All right. Let's have it out. Say whatever you need to say."

She shoves a piece of broccoli into her mouth and leans down to feed a floret to Romeo under the table.

Even the dog hates me right now. He puts his head down whenever I look his way.

"Look, I understand that you're not happy with being grounded, but—"

"This has nothing to do with being grounded!"

Noah's outburst startles me. "Then talk to me. What is this about?"

"You were so mean to Lenny. That was uncalled for, especially after she helped me. If it weren't for her, Romeo wouldn't be here right now."

"No, if it weren't for you not keeping the door closed like I asked you to—"

"I forgot, Dad. I fucking forgot, okay?"

"Whoa, language. You can yell and express your feelings, but you will not start cursing at me."

"I'm sorry but you make me so mad sometimes. I'm not perfect. And neither are you, by the way. I can't be the person you want me to be. I'm going to forget things sometimes. I'm going to mess up. Lenny didn't have to stop and help me today, but she did—even after what I did to her. She drove around the neighborhood looking for Romeo, and she used her leftover steak and lured him back. It was her idea to get the duck to squeak so he'd hear us. She is the reason Romeo is okay, and you treated her like shit."

"Language." I slam my fist on the table. "I know, okay? I know I treated her poorly. But I was mad. And when I get mad, I don't think straight. I know I'm not perfect, and I don't expect you to be perfect either. I just need you to think." I tap my finger against my temple. "I need you to think so that these accidents don't happen. What if Romeo got hit by a car? What if he attacked someone? What if he was gone for good? I'm the one left to pick up the pieces when your heart breaks, and *that's* why I'm so hard on you—because I can't bear to see you hurt."

"Well, you yelling at Lenny hurt me."

I nod, letting her words sink in.

She's right. Tell your daughter she's right.

"I guess I was a little harsh on her."

Noah coughs out an incredulous laugh. "You *guess*? I don't know how she didn't slap you after the way you spoke to her—and you didn't even thank her." She crosses her arms over her chest. "Is that the way you'd want a boy to speak to me?"

Oh, she went there.

I roll my eyes. "Not the same situation."

"You always tell me that a boy should treat me with respect. Do you feel like you showed Lenny respect?"

I clench my jaw. "Who are you, Dr. Phil?"

She rolls her lips between her teeth. "I'm right and you know it."

"Yeah, yeah."

She leans in. "You need to apologize to her."

"No fucking way."

"Language."

I offer her a fake polite smile. "I'm sorry. I meant to say: No *freaking* way."

Noah shakes her head. "I never knew my father was a chickenshit."

"I am *not* a chickenshit."

"Then apologize. Go over there right now and apologize to her."

Blondie's words echo in my mind: *You sure aren't winning any parent of the year awards.* She's not wrong. I've always felt less than as a single parent, especially as the father to a daughter. I don't know what the hell I'm doing most days, and it shows.

"The person I want to apologize to is you." I reach out and cover her hand with mine. "I don't ever want you to feel like you're afraid to mess up around me. I'm your father, and I will love you no matter what mistakes you might make. I don't want you to feel like you're walking on eggshells around me." I shake my head. "My father made me feel that way and I don't want you to grow up feeling like you're not good enough."

"If you want to do better than grandpa, then you need to apologize to people."

I scratch my nails against the scruff on my chin. "Why did I have to raise such a good kid, hmm?"

"Because you're a good dad. That's the one thing Lenny was wrong about."

Affection blooms in my chest, sending a warm current throughout my body. "I'm trying my best, kid."

Noah scoots closer to the table and picks up her fork again. "I like Lenny."

"Do you?"

"Yeah, she's cool. She's really pretty too. I wish my hair could be that shiny."

"Your hair is fine the way it is."

"You're my dad. You have to say that."

I scoff. "You think I wouldn't tell you if you were ugly?"

She laughs around the food in her mouth. "Come on. Admit it. Lenny is super pretty."

I'm not admitting shit…at least not to Noah.

But *pretty* is an understatement for my pain-in-the-ass neighbor. Before our encounter on Halloween, I'd appreciated her beauty from afar. I'd stolen a glance or two, fighting the urge to help her with her lawn when she was overwatering it, or carry in the groceries for her. She talks to everyone in the neighborhood—everyone but me—and as much as that has always bothered me, I know it's for the best. My focus needs to be on my daughter, not the curvy hips and thick thighs across the street.

Noah takes a sip of water and glances at me over the rim of her glass. "She was really nice to me, Dad."

I grunt. "Good. She'd better be."

I BLOW out a long stream of breath through my lips.

Then I reach out and press my finger to the doorbell.

The things we do for kids.

The red door opens wide enough for Blondie to stick out her head. "Is Noah okay?"

"Yeah, she's fine. I—"

The door shuts in my face.

Here we fucking go.

I tap my knuckles against the door this time. "Would you let me say what I came here to say?"

"I don't want to hear anything you have to say."

I pinch the bridge of my nose. "Look, I'm not here to fight."

"Then what do you want?"

"For you to open the door so I can apologize to your face." I glance down at the foil-covered plate in my left hand. "And to give you this peace offering."

The door splits open. Her hair is tied up in a bun on top of her head and her cheeks are tinged with a pretty pink. A black sports bra hugs her chest, propping her tits up like they're on display, and a sliver of her stomach is exposed before disappearing underneath high-waisted spandex pants that cling to her soft curves.

Damn, she is thick and sexy as hell.

"I just got home from the gym and I'm dying to take a shower." She eyes the plate in my hand, her eyes darting from it to me. "What do you want?"

I clear my throat. "Noah said you used your steak to entice Romeo to come to you, so I wanted to replace it."

Her eyebrows hit her hairline. "You made me a steak?"

I nod. "It's still warm. I just put it on the grill."

"And you think I'm going to eat something *you* cooked?" She huffs out a laugh. "What did you do to it? Arsenic? Season it with a laxative? Spit on it? Rub it against the ground? Wipe your ass with—"

"I didn't do anything to it. You can ask Noah."

She takes the plate from me and peels back the foil on one side. "This actually looks good."

"Like I said: It's a peace offering."

She chews her bottom lip before she responds. "Just to be clear, I'm only taking it because I was really looking forward to my leftovers."

"Sure."

She plants one hand on her hip and lifts her chin. "All right. Let's get this apology over with."

My stomach clenches. For some reason, I'm nervous, as if her opinion of my apology matters in the slightest.

It doesn't.

Still, I find myself hoping she accepts it.

I shove my hands into my pockets. "I shouldn't have jumped down your throat when you told me about Noah taking your candy bowl. I wish I would've reacted differently. She's been hanging with the wrong crowd lately, and I don't like how she acts when she's with them. So, when you said she stole something, it was like my fears were coming true and I panicked. Not to make an excuse, but at least you know the real reason I snapped at you.

"I also shouldn't have put the spider in your mailbox, or messed with the backup camera on your car. Honestly, Noah was having so much fun pranking you, I didn't want to stop because at least she was spending time with me and talking to me." I glance down at my shoes. "It's hard raising a teenager." I slip one hand out of my pocket and rub the scruff on my chin, preparing for the last part of my apology. I haven't said the words *I'm sorry* to anyone in so long, I'm not sure how to form them. "I'm...I'm sorry for the way I spoke to you and for the way I've treated you. You didn't deserve any of that."

Blondie leans against the doorframe. "I appreciate your apology. I owe you one too."

My eyebrows lift. "Really?"

"I can be woman enough to say that I didn't handle this situation in the best way. I was angry when you were so rude to me on Halloween. But I had no business sneaking around on your property and stealing Mr.... Whatever His Name Is."

"Mr. Bubbles."

"Yeah, him." She shifts the plate from one hand to the other. "I teach my students to treat others the way they want to be treated, and that's not what I did. So, I'm sorry."

A wave of relief floods me. "Well, it's over then."

She peeks under the foil again. "You really didn't do anything to this?"

"Guess you'll have to take a bite and find out."

"At least your fingerprints will be all over it if I die."

"You're not going to die."

She pauses a moment, letting her eyes bounce between mine. "Noah is a sweet kid. I shouldn't have made a comment about your parenting skills. That was a low blow."

I arch a brow. "You also said that I'm insecure and overcompensating for something."

A playful smile tugs at her lips as she rakes her eyes over me. "Jury is still out on that, I guess."

It sounds like a challenge.

Or maybe I just want it to be.

Which I shouldn't.

I didn't come over here to flirt. I've tortured this woman enough.

I clear my throat. "Enjoy your steak…Lenny?"

"It's short for Elena."

"Well, good night, Elena."

Before I turn around, she sticks out her hand. "Truce?"

I engulf her hand in mine and give her a firm shake. "Truce."

8

ELENA

"Hey, Lenny."

I glance over my shoulder. "Oh, hey, Noah."

She lowers herself onto the bottom porch step and drops her backpack onto the ground. "Whatcha doing?"

"I'm installing a doorbell camera, like you and your dad have." I grunt as I twist the screw into its designated hole. "Or at least I'm trying to."

"Can I help?"

I glance at her house, noting the missing truck in her driveway. "Will your father be okay with this?"

Sure, we've exchanged apologies and called a truce—and he made me a killer steak—but I don't know that Grant wants his daughter to hang out with me, especially if he's not home. We're still strangers.

"As long as I take Romeo on a walk, he'll be okay." She hikes a shoulder. "We're right across the street."

"Take Romeo on that walk first and I'll be here waiting for you."

"Really? You'll let me help?"

"Of course. Maybe you'll have better luck than I've had." I toss the instruction manual onto the rocking chair. "I've been stuck on this one step for the last twenty minutes."

A wide smile breaks onto her face. "Okay, I'll be back in ten."

I chuckle as she bolts across the street. I've never seen someone so excited to help install a doorbell camera.

Where's her mother?

I've lived across the street from them for the last several years, but I've never noticed whether or not Noah has been here on specific days. I've also never seen women going in or out of the house.

Is Grant with anyone?

I shake my head and pick up the manual, forcing myself to focus on the task at hand and not on my hot neighbor's love life—which doesn't concern me in the slightest. Not even after I caught him checking me out in my workout outfit last night. *Goddamn*, that steak was delicious. The man looks like that and he can cook? It doesn't seem fair.

Five minutes later, I realize the manual I'm staring at is upside-down.

"Stop thinking about him, you idiot."

When Noah returns from her walk, she ties Romeo's leash around the railing on my porch. His tail thumps against the grass until I walk over to pet him.

I kneel down and scratch behind his ears. "You're only excited to see me because you think I have steak."

Noah smiles. "My dad's steak was good, wasn't it?"

"It was."

"I know he seems like a big mean ogre, but he's not so bad." Noah shrugs. "He means well. He's just…super serious about everything I do."

"He cares about you a lot." I press a kiss to Romeo's head before standing. "You're lucky."

She nods but says nothing as she picks up the screwdriver and goes to work on the doorbell camera.

I lower myself onto the rocking chair. "My dad was a jerk, and then he died. It just wasn't in him to be the caring, loving father I wanted."

"What about your mom?"

"She's great. She has early-onset Alzheimer's. I visit her at the nursing home every week. In a way, it's like she died too, even though she's still here. It's just not the same."

The screwdriver slips from Noah's hand, and she bends down to snatch it. "I'm sorry. That's…that's really sad."

"It took me some time but I've accepted it." I rest my head against the chair as I rock. "You're not always going to see eye-to-eye with your parents. You'll fight and you'll feel like they don't understand you. But they understand you better than you think. You appreciate them more when you're older, which kind of sucks because in many cases, by then, it's too late."

"My mom died." Noah glances down at Romeo as she talks, her voice barely above a whisper. "I was a baby when she overdosed on a bottle of pills, so I don't remember her at all. Sometimes I miss her, but that's probably stupid because how can I miss someone I never knew, right?"

My chest aches for her. To be a teenage girl without a mom can be difficult. Hell, I'm a grown adult and it sucks without my mom. But I'm also sad for Grant and what he went through raising a baby on his own, and then losing Noah's mother at the same time.

I shake my head. "It's not stupid. You miss the idea of her. You miss what you could've had with her. I feel the same way about my dad."

She slumps down into the wicker chair beside me. "My dad is great, don't get me wrong. But sometimes, I think it'd be nice to have a mom too. It never used to bother me until recently."

"Because you're a teenager. Things are a little different right now."

She nods. "I can't talk to my dad about certain things. He just doesn't understand. He's so…"

"He's a man."

"Yes." Noah lets out a small chuckle. "He's such a man, and everything is so easy for him. He doesn't know what it's like to be me."

"I don't know your father, but I can almost guarantee that he'd understand more than you expect him to." I shrug. "I know it's not the same as having a mom. But he's raised you all this time, and I think he's done a pretty damn good job. Man, woman, mom, dad, it's all the same as long as he loves you."

She gestures to the doorbell. "You had it in upside-down. That's why it wasn't screwing in right."

"Wow. I'm an idiot."

Noah chuckles as she lifts her big brown eyes to meet mine. "I like talking to you."

My chest explodes with warmth. I reach out and clasp Noah's hand. "I like talking to you too. I'm always here if you ever have any girly questions your father can't answer."

"Who says I can't answer girly questions?"

Grant's deep voice startles us both.

Noah jumps to her feet. "Hey, Dad. Look what I did." She gestures to my new doorbell. "Lenny let me install it because she was having some trouble."

"Very nice." Grant's dark eyes flick between the both of us. "How was school?"

Noah and I both answer at the same time. "It was good."

My cheeks burn as I slap my palm against my forehead. "Of course you were talking to your daughter. You don't care about my day. I don't know why I answered. I heard school and thought you were talking about me."

Why do I ramble so much around this man?

"Do you have homework?" Grant rolls his lips between his teeth, failing to suppress a smirk. "This question is for Noah, by the way."

My cheeks flame. *Jerk.*

"Only math." Noah groans. "But I have literally no idea what I'm doing. The teacher goes so fast and—"

"And you're too afraid to ask for help," Grant finishes.

Noah's shoulders droop.

"What kind of math is it?" I raise my right hand. "I'm pretty good with math. I can help if you want."

Grant shakes his head. "That's not necessary. I'm sure you have things to do."

I stare at Noah, waiting for her response.

"Fractions. They're literally the worst thing ever created."

I scrunch my nose. "I used to hate fractions when I was your age. If it's okay with your father, I can help."

Noah blinks up at her father. "Please, Dad? You suck at fractions."

He scoffs. "I do not. I'm just rusty."

She rolls her eyes. "That's because you're old."

"Forty-two is not old."

I bite my lip to keep from laughing. "Did you have paper and pencils back when you were in school, or did you have to scratch your equations onto a cave wall?"

Noah tosses her head back as she laughs.

Grant rests his hands on his hips as he turns to face me, and I fight the urge to stare at the muscles in his arms as they flex. "I knew I should've poisoned that steak."

"You had your chance, big guy. You blew it."

"Come on, Dad. Please? Let Lenny help me."

He heaves a sigh. "At least let me pay you for your tutoring time."

"No way. Don't be silly. I don't mind helping her."

"I insist."

"I won't take your money."

Noah snaps her fingers. "Why don't you cook dinner for her? It's almost dinnertime anyway, and she said she loved your steak."

I don't miss the glare Grant cuts her way.

"I don't want to impose." I adjust the hem of my shirt, suddenly uneasy about the idea of having dinner at Grant's house. "You don't have to feed me."

"Please come." Noah hits me with those big, round puppy eyes. "It'll give me someone else to talk to during dinner."

"Apparently I'm not good enough anymore." Grant lets out another long sigh. "I'm making oven-roasted chicken with potatoes tonight. Is that all right with you?"

"Sure. I'm not picky." I glance down at my button-down shirt and pencil skirt. "Just let me change out of my work clothes and I'll be right over."

Noah throws her arms around me. "Yay! See you soon."

Noah and Romeo trot across the street.

Grant and I remain, staring at one another.

He gestures to my new doorbell. "I thought you said a camera is creepy."

"I changed my mind. Figured it'd be good to have some added security around here. You never know who's lurking around the corner."

He grunts. "Yeah, you should watch out. I heard there's a gnome thief on the loose."

"You make so much sense. Why can't my teacher explain it like this?"

I smile. "He might if you ask him for some help."

Noah shakes her head. "No way. That's so embarrassing. The people in my class will think I'm an idiot."

Grant glances at her over his shoulder from where he stands at the stove. "Who cares what they think? They're not the ones flunking math."

I hold up my hand to stop him from making this any worse. "You don't have to say it to the teacher in front of the whole class. You can go up to him at the end of class and ask him if he offers extra help. I know some teachers who do a lunch bunch. Instead of going to lunch, a couple of times a week you can go to him so he can explain the lesson to you in a smaller setting."

Noah's eyebrows lift. "Really?"

"You can also email him if you're too nervous to ask in person. I don't know any teacher who wouldn't want to extend some extra help to a kid who's asking for it."

"See?" Grant tosses a pot holder onto the middle of the table. "Ask for help. You'll never know if you don't ask."

Noah rolls her eyes behind his back as he turns to face the oven again.

"Here." I tap on the next page in her textbook. "Take these practice questions and then you'll be done."

While she works, I steal a glance at Grant. He towers over the kitchen counter, the span of his wide shoulders stretching the fabric in his dirt-streaked white T-shirt. Though he's in loose-fitting jeans, they're tight around his backside.

This man does *not* skip leg day.

Everything about him is large and thick, and my mind wanders to visions of him lifting weights at the gym. Sweaty. Grunting. Rippling muscles.

A hot flush crawls up my neck and into my cheeks. "Can I please have some water?"

"Your face is red." Noah cocks her head. "Do you want me to open the window?"

"No, that's okay." I avoid eye contact with Grant as he places a water bottle in front of me. "It's probably the heat from the oven."

Or the man standing in front of it.

"Dinner's ready whenever you guys are." Grant places a pan on top of the pot holder on the table.

I pop out of my seat needing to keep busy. "Let me set the table while she finishes her practice quiz."

Grant points to the cabinet to his left. "Plates are in there."

I reach up onto my toes and grab three plates. "Geez, this kitchen is made for a giant."

When I turn back around, Grant's eyes are on my ass. He clears his throat and averts his eyes as if he wasn't checking me out.

But I caught him.

I don't skip leg day either.

"Sorry." He rubs the back of his neck. "I've never invited one of my lawn gnomes to set the table in here before."

Noah coughs out a laugh behind her hand.

"Oh, you think that's funny, kid?" I set a plate in front of her. "Good luck with your math. I might be short but at least I can add fractions."

Grant cocks a brow. "Short and scrappy, huh?"

"I was Black Widow for Halloween, remember?"

He mutters something under his breath as he reaches down to

scoop potatoes onto each plate.

"Finished." Noah slides the book toward me. "I think I got everything correct."

I lean over the table and check her answers. Sure enough, she's golden. "You got it. Awesome job, Noah."

"Woohoo!" She pumps her fist in the air. "You're the best, Lenny."

I scoot into the chair beside her at the small square table, opposing Grant. My eyes bounce around the kitchen as we eat, taking in the simplicity and organization of everything.

"Wow, this chicken is great." I stab another piece and stick it in my mouth. "Where did you learn to cook like this?"

"My mother is a great cook. I used to help her in the kitchen growing up."

"She makes the best pies." Noah talks around a ball of food in her cheek. "I'll save you some on Thanksgiving. You have to taste them."

The fact that Noah is already thinking ahead to Thanksgiving makes me smile. "My mom used to be a good cook too."

Noah frowns as she looks to her dad. "Lenny's mom has early Alzheimer's."

Grant lays his fork down on the table. "I'm sorry to hear that."

"It's okay." I shrug like it's not the most devastating to ever happen to me. "She used to make the best chocolate cake. Now I make it and bring it to the nursing home when I visit."

"Why did you say your dad was a jerk?"

"Noah." Grant holds up a hand. "Excuse my daughter. She has no manners."

Noah's eyes widen. "Dad, she literally said it herself. I'm just asking why."

"It's okay, really. He worked hard and took care of the bills and the house. But he wasn't a family man. He didn't spend time with me, or help me with schoolwork. He said some mean things to me. I was more of a bother to him than anything else." I hike a shoulder. "And then he died, and I didn't know how to feel about it. I still don't. I can't say I missed the good times, because there weren't any. Still, I feel sad that he's gone. It's weird."

"It's not weird." Noah reaches over and clasps my hand. "You miss what you wished you could've had. Just like you told me about my mom."

One corner of my mouth turns up. "You're right."

Grant listens as we talk, his eyes flicking between us, but offers nothing to our conversation. The way he looks at me is as if he's trying to figure me out. He might have invited me into his home, but he's still cautious about me being around his daughter.

Does he ever let his guard down?

Noah scampers off to her room after dinner, and Grant pushes his chair back from the table and carries his plate to the sink.

I stand and stack Noah's plate on mine. "I'll help with the dishes."

"You are not doing the dishes." Grant blocks the sink. "You are a guest, and guests do not do dishes."

"Fine." I give the kitchen one more glance before I turn around. "Thank you for dinner. Seriously, you're a great cook."

"You're welcome here anytime. Noah likes your company."

The invitation warms my chest. But then his words repeat in my head, and I realize: Noah isn't the only one who could use the company.

How long has Grant *really* been alone?

"I should be the one thanking you." Grant clears his throat. "I heard what you were talking about earlier, outside with Noah, that it doesn't matter if I'm a mom or a dad—as long as I love her."

"It's the truth."

He nods. "Good night, Elena."

A small smile blooms on my face as I walk back across the street. And a week ago, I would've never believed that my grumpy neighbor across the street would be the one to put it there.

9

ELENA

The next day, Grant and I set up a schedule for tutoring Noah.

I'll be there three nights a week, and he'll repay me by cooking dinner.

Not a bad deal, if you ask me.

Tonight's menu consists of chicken parmesan and spaghetti, with a side of Grant and Noah arguing.

Again.

"You have an iPad. Why do you need a phone?"

"I can't fit an iPad in my purse, Dad."

"Get a bigger purse."

Noah blows a stream of air through her nostrils. "But everyone has a phone."

"They're not my daughter. You are."

"Don't you want to know where I am? You'd be able to keep tabs on me with a phone."

"I always know where you are." Grant hikes a shoulder. "And your friends' parents have cell phones, so I can contact them."

"I just don't see what the big deal is." Noah turns her attention to me. "Tell him, Lenny. I'm old enough for a phone, don't you think?"

I hold up my hands on either side of my head. "I'm not getting in the middle of this one."

Grant tilts his head. "Do you think I'm being unreasonable?"

I chew my bottom lip. "No…"

"But?"

"But if you gave her a phone, then you could have her location god forbid something happens. There won't always be a parent there to supervise her." I shrug. "If I had a kid, I'd want her to have a phone."

He stares down at his plate while he chews.

"Why don't you have any kids?" Noah asks.

I set myself up for that one, didn't I?

"I wanted to, but that wasn't in the cards for me."

"Do you have a husband? Or a boyfriend?"

Grant watches me as his daughter asks what's on her mind. "That's enough questions, Noah."

She drops her chin. "I'm just asking."

I lean both elbows onto the table. "You can ask me anything you want. It's okay." I force a smile. "I did have a husband, but now he's my ex-husband. And I don't have a boyfriend."

"Why did you guys get divorced?"

"Well, uh, he cheated on me. And now they're engaged and she's having his baby."

Grant chokes on his water.

Noah scrunches her nose. "Eww. What an asshole."

"Language," comes from both me and Grant.

She hikes a shoulder. "Sorry, but it's true."

Grant nods. "The guy does sound like an asshole."

Noah beams. "See?"

"Since our divorce, I've been too nervous to get back into the dating scene, so I'm taking this time for myself." I slap my palm against my forehead. "That sounds pretty lame when I say it out loud."

"That's not lame. Dad is single too. He hasn't dated anyone in for-ev-er."

Grant ignores Noah's comment, but redness creeps into his cheeks.

"There was one woman, like, a long time ago," she continues. "But she was weird."

Grant drops his fork. "She wasn't weird."

Noah shoots him a dubious look. "She had an ant farm in her house."

He picks up his fork again and shoves a mound of potatoes into his mouth.

"Exactly." Noah returns her attention to me. "I was five and terrified of bugs, and this woman was living with them inside of her home."

I stifle a laugh. "Everyone is into different things. I'm sure she was a nice person."

"Ants, Lenny." Noah's eyes are wide. "The woman was harvesting ants. I don't care how nice you are. One wrong move, and you're being carried away to the ant queen."

A laugh escapes me as the visual assaults my mind.

Grant glares at me, but amusement dances in his eyes. "That was the first and last time I let my friends put me on a dating app."

"She wasn't hot enough to overlook the ants, huh?"

He rolls his lips between his teeth. "I had a five-year-old clinging to my leg, refusing to sit in the same room as her because she thought she brought the ants with her in her purse. It wasn't going to work."

"Yeah, right. Blame it on me." Noah rolls her eyes. "The woman was nuts."

He looks uncomfortable talking about this, so I try to take the heat off him. "What about you, Noah?" I waggle my eyebrows. "Got your eye on any hotties at school?"

Grant chimes in right away. "Yeah, any necks I have to break?"

She looks truly horrified, mouth open and eyes wide. "Oh my god, no. We are not having this conversation."

"For someone who has so many questions, you sure don't like to talk about your personal life." Grant pokes her arm with his fork. "Spill the beans. What boys have asked you to make out under the bleachers?"

"Or girls," I add.

Grant pauses. "I'd prefer that."

"The bleachers?" Noah screeches. "It's not 1976."

"When does your family life class start?" Grant's fork clanks against his dish. "Did it start already?"

Noah buries her face in her hands. "Dad…"

"Did you learn about sex yet?"

"Oh my god, stop!" Noah jumps up from her seat. "I am leaving this room right now. I've suddenly lost my appetite."

She runs out of the room like it's on fire.

My head tilts back as I laugh and clutch my stomach. "I think we just traumatized her."

Grant grins. "I've never seen her run so fast."

Holy shit. Grant Harper is smiling.

I sober as my eyes fixate on his face. Slight dimples bracket his mouth and the corners of his eyes crinkle as his wide smile pushes up his cheeks. His eyes shine like black obsidian stones. And his deep laughter reverberates in my chest, spreading goose bumps along my skin.

Forget his ass. Forget all of his muscles. His smile—that's the most mesmerizing sight.

"You know, I've noticed you across the street for years and I don't think I've ever seen you smile."

He clears his throat and the smile fades. "You've noticed me?"

Heat crawls into my chest. "Kind of hard not to, if I'm being honest."

He keeps his eyes locked with mine, and I'd give just about anything to hear what he's thinking.

But he doesn't let me in on whatever it is.

I want to make him smile again. "What do you call a fish wearing a bowtie?"

His eyebrows press together. "What?"

"Come on, guess. What do you call a fish wearing a bowtie."

His eyes roam my face while he thinks. "I don't know."

"So-fish-ticated."

One corner of his mouth twitches.

I grin. "Okay, how about: If April showers bring May flowers, what do May flowers bring?"

He arches a brow.

"Pilgrims."

He rolls his lips.

"Nothing? Really?" I rub my palms together. "Fine. Okay, here's my favorite: Why did Snoop Dogg grab his umbrella?"

Grant tilts his head.

"You do know who Snoop Dogg is, right?"

He rolls his eyes. "Yes, I know who he is. Now tell me why he grabbed his umbrella."

I waggle my eyebrows. "Fo' drizzle."

Grant laughs into his hand and covers it up with his hand.

"Yes!" I pump my fists into the air. "I did it!"

He shakes his head as he balls up his napkin and drops it onto his plate. "Those are pretty painful jokes."

"Painfully hilarious." I nudge his elbow. "Come on, you're a dad. You need to brush up on your dad jokes."

"I'll get right on that."

I help Grant clear off the table, and thank him for dinner.

Tonight, he walks me out onto the porch.

His eyes trail across the street. "I can help you with your lawn if you'd like."

My nose scrunches. "My lawn?"

He slips his hands into his pockets. "It helps if you winterize the grass before the temperature really drops. Now's the time to do it so you're not having such a hard time with it in the spring."

Why is he talking about my lawn?

Then it hits me.

I've struggled to keep my grass green, and I spend a lot of time outside in the spring and summer months, putting down fertilizer and watering it, trying to will it back to life.

Something a neighbor would notice me doing.

I bite my bottom lip to keep the smile from spreading across my face. "Sure, I'd love some help."

I told Grant I've noticed him…

But he just told me he's noticed me too.

10

GRANT

"I'm going to fail."

Elena squeezes Noah's hand. "We've only been practicing for a week. It's okay if you fail."

Noah rests her forehead on the table. "But I don't want to get grounded."

I set down the pot on the stove and turn to face Noah. "I only grounded you that one time because you didn't study. Not because you failed. I see how hard you've been practicing for this test though. I'd never ground you for that."

Elena nods. "And we can look at the questions you might get wrong, and figure out what's still confusing you. We learn when we make mistakes. I tell my students that tests are a celebration of knowledge. It shows them everything they've learned, and where they need to practice more."

"I like that." Noah lifts her head and offers her a small smile. "A celebration of knowledge."

Leave it to Blondie to turn a failing grade into a celebration.

Elena grips her shoulders. "But let's not assume the worst, right? Think positive and believe in yourself. You've been doing great on all these practice tests. I bet you'll pass this test next week."

"I have been working really hard. I deserve a little reward."

Noah shoots me an innocent look. "So, can I go to the mall with Hannah tonight?"

My chin jerks back. "What do you need to go to the mall for?"

"We go to hang out."

"I worked my ass off all day *and* cooked dinner. Have you done any of your chores this week? Cleaned your room or done any laundry? Maybe run a vacuum around the floor and suck up all this dog hair." I glare at Romeo, who hides his face under his paw as if he understands me.

Noah's shoulders slump. "No, but I will."

I scrub my hand over my jaw. "You're going to do all your chores right now?"

"Yes." She pops up out of her seat. "Give me an hour. Then can you drive me to the mall?"

I swallow a groan. "No. My back is killing me and the last thing I want to do is play chauffeur."

"If you'd go to the doctor for your back like I keep telling you to, maybe this wouldn't be an issue." Noah stomps her foot before storming out of the room.

Elena opens her mouth to say something, but I hold up one finger. "Wait for it."

Upstairs, a door slams shut.

"Ah, there it is." I lower myself onto the chair she abandoned. "She's going to slam that door off the hinges one day."

Elena folds her hands on the table. "I'll take her and her friend to the mall."

"No. No way. I can't ask you to do that."

"You're not asking. I'm offering." She shrugs like it's no big deal. "I have to get a couple of things for my best friend's wedding next weekend anyway. I'll walk around and do some shopping until they're ready to leave."

"You don't need to do this."

She nudges me with her elbow. "Come on. She deserves some teenage fun with her friends, and you deserve a night off from dad duty."

I stare down at my hands in my lap. I do prefer the thought of an adult being with Noah while she's out with her friend. And if Elena is going to the mall anyway...

"You really don't mind?"

She shakes her head. "Not at all."

"That's very kind of you."

Who would've thought we'd end up on friendly terms after the way things started?

One second, we're at each other's throats, and the next, she's in my home, eating my food, helping my daughter.

Getting under my skin.

I lift my eyes to hers. "Your little *celebration of knowledge* put a positive spin on this upcoming test. I never seem to have the right words to say to her."

"I'm a teacher. That's what I do."

"You're not like any of the teachers I've had."

In more ways than one.

She smirks. "That's because teachers were different in your generation. Did you get smacked around with a ruler?"

"That was my father's generation. I'm not *that* old."

Her smirk turns into a full-blown grin, and it makes something tighten in my chest.

"How old *are* you, Elena?"

"Twenty-nine."

Damn. Thirteen years apart sounds bad when you say it out loud.

I shake my head. "I guess that does make me old."

"Oh, please. You're hotter than any forty-two-year-old I've ever seen." Her eyes widen as they snap up to mine. "I mean, shit, I shouldn't have said that. I don't know where that came from. I'm sorry. I just meant...well, you're a handsome man and you probably know it. I'm sure women tell you that all the time. I didn't mean to make things weird. We're adults though, right? I should be able to tell you that you're a DILF." She puts her hands up as if to stop herself, yet she keeps going. "I totally didn't mean that in a literal way. I'm not saying I want to, you know, but that's what you're called when you're a hot dad, so I was just saying—" She cuts herself off and yells upstairs. "Noah, come down here please."

I can barely make out any of her incoherent babbling, but I definitely don't miss the part where she called me hot.

And I can't pretend like that doesn't affect me.

Noah's feet pound on the stairs and then she skids into the kitchen.

Elena pops up out of her chair, almost knocking the thing over. "I'm going to drive you to the mall. You can get your coat and meet me outside."

Noah scrunches her nose. "Okay. Why are you acting weird?"

"Weird? I'm not acting weird." Elena's eyes dart to me and then back to Noah. "I'm fine. Your dad is fine—but not fine as in *hot*—just like, regular fine. We're all fine here. Everything is fine."

Jesus, this woman is nuts when she's nervous.

It's adorable.

I cross my arms over my chest and tilt my head.

Her eyes dart between the two of us. "Okay, bye."

Noah stares after her as she bolts out the door. "What the heck?"

"Don't ask." I pinch the bridge of my nose. "Make sure you're home by nine o'clock. Not a minute later, you understand?"

"Got it." Noah salutes me. "Thank you, Dad. You're the best."

"Thank your lunatic driver. It was her idea."

Noah smiles. "She's great, isn't she?"

I grunt.

Yeah. She really fucking is.

Elena

"Are you coming in?"

I shake my head. "I'm going to call it a night."

Noah turns to face me in the passenger seat. "I never saw what you bought at the mall."

"Just a pair of shoes and a pretty necklace. My best friend is getting married next weekend."

She crinkles her nose. "Do you have to wear an ugly bridesmaid dress?"

"Nope. I got to pick out my own dress and it is fabulous."

"Weddings always look so fun on TV. Will there be a DJ?"

"Yup."

Noah stares out the windshield at her house. "Dad never gets invited to weddings."

"He's older. His friends might already be married."

"He never sees his friends very often." Her lips tug down into a frown. "I feel like he has no life because of me."

I cover her hand with mine. "It's not because of you. He works a grueling job. He's probably tired. And the free time he does have, he wants to spend it with you."

Noah hums. "I guess."

The front door opens and Grant steps out onto the porch wearing a black T-shirt with gray sweatpants.

I try to suck the drool back into my mouth before Noah catches it.

Gray sweatpants get me every time.

"Dad, Elena is going to a wedding. How come we never go to weddings?"

"Do you know anyone getting married?"

"No."

"Me neither."

I chuckle as I step outside. "My friend gave me a plus one to the wedding, but I don't have anyone to take with me. If it's okay with you, maybe Noah could be my date?"

Noah gasps. "Oh my god, Dad. You *have* to let me go to the wedding."

He arches a dark brow at me. "You sure you want her tagging along?"

I wave a hand. "Please, she'll help me have fun. Every one of my friends is coupled up, so I've been the third wheel since my divorce. I'm dreading having to sit on the sidelines during all the slow dances."

He glances at Noah. "You don't have anything to wear."

"I have some old dresses in my closet," I offer. "We can see what fits her."

Noah's eyes widen. "Can you do my hair and makeup too?"

Grant holds up a hand. "Whoa. No one said anything about makeup."

"Please, Dad? Weddings are fancy. I have to wear makeup."

His shoulders rise and fall as he exhales. "Fine."

Noah screeches. "I have to go call Hannah. She's going to be so jealous."

"Brush your teeth and get ready for bed," he calls after her.

"Got it!" she yells back before she disappears inside the house.

I grimace. "Sorry, I didn't mean to spring this on you. I should've asked you first."

"It's fine. It'll make her happy." His eyes hold mine as the silence stretches between us. "You know, she doesn't have a lot of women to look up to in her life."

"I hope you know how seriously I take that. And that you're letting me spend time with her. I know that might not be easy for you." I hold out my phone. "If you give me your number, I can send you pictures throughout the night of the wedding. This way you're not worried sick, wondering how she's doing."

"I'd appreciate that very much." He puts his number into my phone and sends a text to himself. "I know she'll be fine, but—"

"But you're her dad, and you're going to worry. I get it." I snap my fingers. "Oh, and just so you know, I don't drink, so you don't have to worry about me being impaired while I'm with her or anything."

"You don't drink at all?"

I shake my head. "My dad drank a lot growing up, so I was never into it."

His frown deepens. "He should've been better for you."

"It's okay. My mom was good enough for the both of them." I reach out and give his shoulder a squeeze. "Just like you are for Noah."

"I don't know that I'm as good as two parents."

"You don't give yourself enough credit." I lower my voice. "Can I ask...what happened to Noah's mother?"

He runs his hand through his hair as his eyes dart to the house. "I don't like to talk about her."

"Of course. But Noah seemed to know a little bit about her when she brought her up to me the other day, so I was just curious..."

I have questions. Noah must have them too.

Were they in love?
Was she an addict when they met?
Did he try to help her?
How could she leave her baby girl like that?

"She knows she was an addict, and she knows that she died. But I haven't gone into too much detail." He glances down at the grass. "I don't really know how to explain it all. She's so young."

I nod. "You'll know when the time is right. It's not easy to have these conversations, but what matters is that she knows she can come to you and ask questions. Communication is important, especially at this age." Our chat the other day comes to the forefront of my mind. "She's at a really pivotal time in her life and she's going to experience some...changes."

"I don't think I'm equipped for this phase." His eyes stay trained on his hands like he's deep in thought. "There's so much I don't know. So much I can't help her with."

I lean forward and grip his hand. "Hey, look at me. You're going to be okay. Nobody knows what they're doing. There's no perfect parent. As long as you love her and you're here for her, that's all that matters in the end. And I can answer any questions you might not know. Not that you need me. I'm sure you have a family and friends too. I'm just saying..."

"Thank you." His frown deepens as she stares at our clasped hands. "She likes having you around."

"You say it like it's a bad thing."

He shakes his head and meets my eyes. "I'm hesitant to let new people into her life."

"People are going to come in and out of her life as she grows up. Not everyone is meant to stay. But they're all meant to teach her a lesson."

He gives me a dubious look, like he doesn't believe me.

"Your ex had a purpose. She gave you Noah. And despite how it ended, I'd say it was worth it."

His thumb grazes my skin, brushing back and forth across the top of my hand. "I love that kid so much it hurts."

Emotion constricts my throat, making it hard to swallow like it always does whenever someone talks about his love for his child.

"I know you do." I squeeze his hand. "You're both so lucky to have each other."

"Maybe the reason Noah had to steal your candy bowl was so that you could be in her life."

"Maybe."

That's a sweet notion, one I didn't expect coming from him.

I turn to walk back to my car, but Grant tugs my hand, not letting it go.

"Regardless of the reason, I'm glad you're here, Elena."

My skin prickles with awareness, heat pooling in my chest. "I'm glad you let me be."

11

ELENA

My stomach clenches as I pull into my driveway, my eyes on the man leaning against the silver BMW parked in front of my house.

I could put the car in reverse and drive away. I don't *have* to face him.

But that won't make him go away.

With a groan, I swing open my car door and step outside. "Hi, Neil. What can I do for you on this lovely day?"

He pushes off the car and walks across my grass. "You haven't answered any of my calls or texts."

"And I don't have to. That's the beauty of divorce."

"I feel like you're ignoring me on purpose. And I get it. I do."

"Do you?" I pause by the mailbox, tapping my finger against my chin. "Tell me, when were you cheated on by your spouse? I didn't realize you'd be able to commiserate."

He runs a hand through his hair. "Don't be difficult, Len."

I cough out an incredulous laugh. "Difficult? You're the one stalking me right now. This is my house, and I have every right to be here for as long as I want."

"I need the money. Half of this house is mine, and I'm ready to sell it."

"Well, I'm not." I push into his space and poke his chest with my index finger. "You don't get to tell me when I sell this house. I could live here forever if I want to, and you won't see a dime from it."

He clenches his jaw. "You're not listening to reason. This house is too big for you living here all by yourself."

"The paperwork says that you get half of the house *if and when* I sell. You showing up here to harass me over it isn't part of the contract."

He rolls his eyes. "Oh, stop being dramatic. I'm not harassing you."

"You're showing up at my house—my house, not yours—trying to bully me into selling this house just so you can get half. What's the matter, you need to buy a ring for Melanie? You two going to get married so you can fuck around on her too?"

He strides toward me, and I slip off the curb trying to back away. I bounce onto my ass and Neil doesn't even offer me a hand to help me up.

I glare up at him, but his eyes widen as he backs up a couple of steps.

The next thing I know, I'm being lifted off the ground and set on my feet.

"Are you okay?" Two large hands cup either side of my face, and I blink up into dark-brown eyes.

"Grant?"

"Tell me you're hurt so I can break this guy's wrist."

"I...I'm fine. What are you doing here?"

He spins around and shields me behind him. "Get back in your stupid fucking car and drive away. Now."

Neil holds his hands up in front of him. "I'm just having a conversation with my ex-wife. This doesn't concern you."

Grant's eyes darken.

Oh, shit.

Grant stalks toward him and grips the collar of his shirt. "I come home and find her on the ground with you standing over her? I'd say that concerns me a whole-fucking-lot."

"I didn't lay a finger on her. She slipped off the curb and—"

"And *you're* what she was backing away from when she fell. So, here's what I'm going to do." Grant drags Neil into the street, still holding onto his collar. "I'm going to give you five seconds to get back into your car and get the fuck out of here. After five seconds, I won't be so generous with my patience." He slams Neil against his driver's side door. "Five…"

"You don't understand why I'm here. I'm just trying to—"

"Four."

"If you would listen—"

"Three."

"Fine. Jesus." Neil swings open his door and Grant helps him by stuffing him inside the car and slamming his door shut.

Grant folds his arms over his chest, unmoving like a statue, until Neil drives away—not before flipping us both off like a pussy.

I hug my midsection as I steady my breaths. "Grant, you didn't have to do that. He's all bark and no bite. He's just a pathetic piece of—"

"Are you all right?" Grant rushes toward me and holds me out in front of him as his eyes scan my body, like he's looking for any obvious signs of injury. "Did you hurt anything when you fell?"

"I'm fine." I look down at my scratched-up palms. "Really, this is it."

He bends my left arm and gestures to my elbow. "This is fine? You're fucking bleeding, Elena."

"It's okay. It's just a scrape. I'll put a Band-Aid on it."

"You have to disinfect it first." He wraps his arm around my shoulders. "Come on. I'll patch you up."

I almost let out a laugh. I tripped off the curb, yet he's acting like I've been shot.

It's adorable.

He leads me into his house and scolds Romeo as he jumps up to greet me. "Down, boy. Not now."

"Hi, Romeo." I pat his head before Grant pulls me into the bathroom.

He gestures to the sink. "Sit."

"Yes, sir." I stifle a laugh as I hop up onto the counter. "You're extra bossy when you're concerned."

And I kind of like it.

He's quiet while he works and I don't mind because it gives me plenty of time to look at him. His large calloused hands are so delicate and careful with me. Long lashes frame his stony eyes. Plump, soft lips surrounded by scratchy stubble. There's a big caring heart underneath the solid muscle. This man is an oxymoron.

"Why are you staring at me?" His voice is low as he dabs a cotton ball against my cut.

"Because you're nice to stare at." My cheeks burn as the words slip out, but I don't regret them.

His eyebrows press together as he covers the gauze on my elbow with medical tape. "Why was he here?"

I roll my eyes and wave a dismissive hand. "If I sell my house, he's entitled to half of it."

"You're moving?"

"No, no. But he thinks he can bully me into moving so he can have his portion of the money. He thinks I'm keeping it from him on purpose, but in reality, I love my house. I don't want to move."

"You should get a restraining order."

"It's not like that. He won't do anything to hurt me."

Grant lifts my elbow. "You're already hurt."

"That was an accident."

Grant crosses his arms over his chest. "He has no right to show up whenever he feels like it. He's harassing you, Elena. You need to put a stop to it."

"A restraining order sounds so…serious."

"What happened out there? That was serious. And it'll keep happening. At the very least, you should put it on file that he's been bothering you. Better safe than sorry."

He's right. I downplay things like they're not a big deal.

"Neil always told me I was *dramatic and too much.*"

"You are neither of those things." Grant tips my chin. "You are the perfect amount of you."

Tears well behind my lids as his words wrap around my heart.

"Please don't cry," he whispers.

"That was the nicest thing anyone's ever said to me."

"You should hear it often."

A tear slips free and then Grant wraps his arms around me and surrounds me in a hug.

I bury my face in his chest. His body wedges between my legs and I wrap them around his waist, holding onto him like a koala hugging a tree.

It feels so damn good in his embrace. Warm and safe. Cared for. It's a feeling I haven't felt in a long time.

I'm scared to feel this.

To enjoy it.

Get it together, Len. He's just being nice. It doesn't mean anything more than a hug between friends.

I sniffle as I pull back. "Neil is just annoying, and I hate feeling like I'm tied to him. Sometimes, it makes me want to sell my house just to get out from under him. I wish I could pay him off and be done but I don't have the money yet."

His thumb swipes away a tear from my cheek. "What can I do?"

"Nothing. It's okay. He doesn't come around that often."

Grant gives me a knowing look. "That's why you installed the camera, isn't it?"

I nod once.

His jaw clenches. "If he bothers you again, I want you to tell me."

"I don't want you to get involved in my mess."

"Too late. I'm involved now. And you will tell me the next time he contacts you. Do you understand?"

With my legs still wrapped around him and his massive presence in my space, I lose my senses. Desire seeps into my bloodstream, coursing through me like a lustful poison.

"Say it, Elena." His gravelly voice rolls over me, causing a wave of goosebumps along my skin. He gazes down at me from under hooded lids, his eyes flicking to my mouth as he runs his thumb over my bottom lip. "Tell me you understand."

"Yes, sir." I skate my tongue across my lip, grazing the tip of his thumb before pulling back. "I understand."

His shoulders rise and fall with his erratic breaths. He moves a fraction of an inch closer to me, brushing his nose against mine. My body is on fire, my most sensitive spot pressed against the growing bulge in his pants. It's taking all my willpower not to roll my hips against him and relieve the ache throbbing between my legs.

Does he want this as much as I do?

As if he can hear my thoughts, his hands slide down my ribs and grip my hips, holding me in place. I can't tell if he's going to grind me against his erection or push me away.

The front door bangs open and Noah's voice shouts through the house. "Dad, I passed my test! We have to tell Lenny."

Grant snaps out of his lustful daze and backs away from me, adjusting his pants before leaving me alone in the bathroom.

"You're about to be a married woman tomorrow. How does it feel?"

"It's surreal." Simone's eyes glisten as she presses her hand to her chest. "I can't believe I'm this basic bitch crying over her wedding."

I laugh. "You're not a basic bitch. This is one of the happiest, most life-changing events in your life. You'd better be crying."

She shakes her head. "Tomorrow is all about me. Let's talk about you tonight. What's new?"

My eyes roam around the restaurant. "Neil showed up at my house today."

"What?"

"He was waiting outside his car when I got home from work. He was trying to convince me to sell the house."

Simone grits her teeth. "He can't do that. That's harassment. What did you say?"

"I told him to go home, and while he was walking toward me, I backed away and tripped off the curb." I hold up my scabbed elbow. "I feel like an idiot."

"Did he put his hands on you?"

"No, no." A slight smirk pulls at one corner of my mouth. "Grant did though."

She gasps. "Grant was there?"

"He came out of nowhere. One second, I was on the ground, and the next thing I knew, he was dragging Neil back to his car."

She covers her mouth with her hand. "Oh, shit. I would've loved to have seen the look on Neil's stupid face when Grant showed up."

"I haven't heard from him since." I roll my eyes. "I know he's not gone forever. Grant thinks I should file a restraining order against him."

"I agree."

"He won't leave me alone until I sell the house."

"*If* you sell the house." Simone reaches for her iced tea and takes a sip. "You don't have to sell. Ever. You can die in that house and he can't have anything to say about it. File the restraining order. I'll go with you."

I nod. "Thanks."

"So, how's everything between you and Grant?"

My cheeks burn, and I bite my bottom lip to keep from smiling like a goof. "I…we…"

Her eyes widen. "Oh my god. What happened?"

"We may or may not have almost kissed today."

She screeches. "You what? Tell me everything."

As I tell her about the way Grant cared for me in the bathroom after the confrontation with Neil, my phone vibrates in my purse. I pull it out and click on the text from Grant.

Grant: I think someone misses you.

I ENLARGE the picture and tilt my head back as I laugh.

I turn the phone to face Simone. "Look how cute this dog is. He's sitting in my chair at Grant's kitchen table."

"*Your* chair, huh?"

I smirk. "It's the chair I usually sit in when I'm at Grant's house."

"Which is every day…while he cooks you dinner."

"He cooks for me because I'm tutoring his daughter, and I refuse to let him pay me."

Tonight is the first weeknight we haven't had dinner together in a while, and I'd be lying if I said I'm not sad about missing it.

"That text right there?" She gestures to my phone. "That's not about the dog missing you. And you know it. You should talk to him, Len. Tell Grant how you feel, and see if he feels the same."

"I don't even know how I feel."

"Yes, you do. I can see it in your eyes when you talk about him. You're starting to have feelings for him."

"I'm attracted to him, for sure. He's a good dad. He works hard."

"Your heart speeds up when you're with him, and your face lights up when he texts you." She arches a brow. "Try to deny it."

I groan and prop up my head with my hand as I lean my elbow onto the table. "I know. You're right."

I like Grant.

I shoot him a text back, not wanting to leave him hanging.

Me: Give him a kiss for me and tell him he's a good boy.
Grant: Someone else misses you too.

I smile down at the picture of Noah sticking out her bottom lip.

Me: Give her a kiss for me too.
Me: And one for yourself while you're at it.
Grant: You'd kiss a mean old ogre?
Me: I'd do a lot of things to that mean old ogre.

. . .

It's a bold text, but I'm not ashamed to put myself out there.

The ball is in his court now. I slip my phone back into my purse, squeezing my thighs together to relieve the ache between them.

Simone sits back against her chair and purses her lips.

"I know, I know. I've got it bad."

"Yeah, you do. And he's obviously into you too. You don't text like that with someone you're strictly platonic with."

"I guess, but he hasn't said anything." I shrug. "He isn't very... expressive with his feelings."

Simone stirs the iced tea with her straw. "You should talk to him. Ask him where his head is at and see how he feels."

My stomach twists at the thought. "Noah said he hasn't dated anyone in a long time, and he said himself that he needs to focus on his daughter."

"Pfft." Simone waves a hand. "She'll be fine. I bet she'd be ecstatic if you dated Grant."

I can't help the smile that spreads across my face. "She's great."

"I have to run to the bathroom. I'll be right back."

"Again?" I glance at her half-empty cup. "Slow down on the liquids. I think you're plenty hydrated."

She laughs. "You can never be too hydrated."

While Simone is in the bathroom, I send Grant an old picture of myself from prom.

Me: This is the dress I have in mind for Noah tomorrow.
Grant: Hell no.
Me: You don't like it?
Grant: I do. Which is why she can't wear it.
Me: It'll look more appropriate on her. Her chest is much smaller than mine was at that time.
Grant: No kidding.
Me: Are you staring at my boobs, sir?
Grant: I think we both know the answer to that.

. . .

I FIGHT to keep the features on my face even when Simone comes back from the bathroom. But something is different about her. She looks worried.

Simone picks at her thumbnail. "Hey, listen. I have to talk to you about something."

My eyes snap to hers. "Okay..."

"Remember when I said I was supposed to get my period the day of my wedding?"

"Did you get it?"

She shakes her head. "And I won't be getting it for a while."

For a while?

I glance at her glass of iced tea, and it hits me. "Oh my god. Simone..."

Her bottom lip trembles. "I don't want to upset you, but you're my best friend, and I need to share this with you."

I jump out of my chair and wrap my arms around her. "I could never be upset. You're having a baby."

"I haven't told anyone yet." She buries her head in my shoulder and sniffles. "This wasn't part of the plan. It's too soon. We're just getting married."

"That's okay." I rub her back in soothing circles. "You've been together since you were in high school, and you're both settled in your careers. It's the perfect time for a baby."

She pulls back and her eyes bounce between mine. "You're not mad?"

"Why the hell would I be mad?" I brush the tears off her cheeks. "Is that what you were worried about?"

Her shoulders slump as she nods. "I know this is difficult for you."

I grip her face. "Listen to me: I can't have kids and that will always make me sad. But that doesn't put a damper on my best friend having a baby. This is a happy moment. Do you understand?"

She nods and another tear falls. "You're going to be a godmother."

Emotion constricts my throat. "And you're going to be a mom."

She wraps her arms around me, and we cry while everyone around us stares. I point at Simone and shout, "My best friend is pregnant!"

People cheer and clap, and Simone laughs. "I guess I have to tell my mother now that everyone in The Cheesecake Factory knows."

I arch a brow. "You know she's going to start buying things as soon as you tell her."

"Which is why I was holding off." She shakes her head. "I am not ready to start planning. I just got done planning a wedding."

"You have time. I'll help you with whatever you need. You just let me know when you're ready."

"You're a good friend, Len." She covers my hand with hers. "You deserve to be happy. You should talk to Grant and see where things go."

There's a reason for everything, and I can't help but think that maybe Grant and I crossed paths because of this very reason. I can't have a child, and he already has his own. One of the reasons I've shied away from dating after my divorce is because men my age are looking to create a family. It's awkward telling them that I can't have kids on the first date, yet I wouldn't want to waste anyone's time.

Maybe this is the perfect situation for me.

Maybe we're perfect for each other.

Maybe Grant is waiting for me to make the first move.

Maybe I should.

Maybe I will.

AT THE END of the night, I drive home without turning on the radio, needing the silence so I can calm the racing thoughts in my head.

I toss my purse onto the entryway table when I get into the house and shed my coat as I head upstairs. I kick off each shoe and change into my cozy sweats. Then I bury myself under the covers in bed.

And I cry.

I let it all out.

I'd never let Simone see this. She deserves to be happy and not feel an ounce of guilt or try to suppress it for me. It's not her fault. It's not mine either. Life happens without regard for anyone's feelings, and we have to roll with it. I knew this day would come. I knew I'd have to watch my best friend have a baby. And I knew it'd hurt.

But knowing it doesn't make it hurt any less.

When I turn off the lamp on my nightstand, a text from Grant pops up on my screen.

GRANT: What does the Gingerbread Man use to make his bed?

I wipe my eyes with the back of my hand and smile as I type out a response.

Me: I don't know…
　Grant: A cookie sheet.
　Me: *laughing emoji*
　Me: That was good.
　Grant: Goodnight, Elena
　Me: Night *kiss emoji*

12

ELENA

"Close your eyes."

"Okay, they're closed."

"Don't open them until we tell you to," Noah shouts.

"Got it."

Noah stifles a laugh. "He's so not into this. He hates surprises."

"He's going to love this one."

Noah heads downstairs on wobbly legs. If we had more time, I'd have made her practice walking in her heels.

My old prom dress fits her perfectly. The stretchy royal-blue material hugs her slim frame, and the crisscross straps in the back made it easy for me to adjust to her small bust. It's simple yet elegant.

When we get downstairs, I nudge Noah's shoulder. "Okay, give your dad a countdown."

"Three, two, one." Noah wrings her hands in front of her. "Open your eyes."

Grant blinks and then his jaw drops open. "Wow."

Noah wraps her arms around herself. "What's wrong?"

"Nothing is wrong." He pushes off my couch and takes slow steps toward her. "You look so grown."

"Doesn't she look beautiful?" I shoot him a prompting look. "Blue looks great on her."

"The dress is super comfy. And not too much makeup, right?" Noah tilts her chin and bats her eyelashes. "Look how long my lashes look."

"I love it, Noah." He reaches out and takes her hands in his. "You look absolutely beautiful. You always look beautiful to me."

Hot tears spring into my eyes. *Shit, now is not the time to test out my waterproof makeup.* I need to save my tears for the wedding.

Noah smiles while an adorable blush creeps into her cheeks. "You're my dad. You're supposed to say that."

"Not true." I raise my hand as I interject. "My father never told me I was beautiful growing up. So, take the compliment and appreciate your dad."

Noah's head jerks back. "Are you crying?"

"No." I dab the corner of my eye with my finger. "There's something in my eye. I haven't dusted in a while. Maybe it's allergies."

Noah slips her phone out of the silver clutch I loaned her. "I'm going to FaceTime Hannah."

I grab the car keys off my end table and toss them to her. "You can wait in the car. I just have to make sure I have everything."

Grant watches me as Noah hobbles outside. "You okay?"

I roll my eyes as I smile. "Yeah, I'm fine. It's really sweet seeing you with Noah. Your approval means a lot to her even though she might not show it."

A frown tugs the corners of his lips. "She's growing up too fast."

"They always do."

Grant's eyes hold mine as he walks backward, stepping away from me. Then his gaze drops, sliding down my body as he makes a slow perusal.

My stomach clenches and my skin prickles with awareness.

The cowl-neck on my satin dress accentuates my chest, and the slit in the long maroon material hits high on my thigh, revealing a sliver of bare skin.

His Adam's apple bobs before he blinks back up to my face. "You look stunning, by the way."

"Thank you." I twirl in a circle. "Not bad for a lawn gnome, huh?"

"Prettiest damn gnome I've ever seen."

Butterfly wings flap against my chest as if a whole garden of them were set loose inside me.

But I stamp them down and laugh it off as I breeze past him. "I don't know. Mr. Bubbles is quite the looker."

Grant

I blink down at my phone and thumb through the pictures Elena sent while I wait for her to arrive.

I cleaned the bathrooms, changed the sheets on both beds, vacuumed upstairs and downstairs. I tried watching a movie but I couldn't tell you which one it was because I was too busy staring at my phone the whole time.

I didn't have to worry about how Noah was doing, or wonder if she was having a good time. Elena snapped picture after picture, updating me on everything Noah did. It's more than I could've asked for after spending the evening away from her.

Some of the pictures were taken by Noah though. She must've had Elena's phone during the ceremony, and she caught a few good shots of Elena crying while her friend exchanged her vows, and Elena entering the reception with her hands above her head. She also sent a hilarious photo of Elena dodging the bouquet, surrounded by a group of women who were fighting for it.

But my favorite is a selfie she took with Elena on the dance floor. Noah's smile is so bright, it reminds me of the little girl she used to be. I can't remember the last time I've seen her smile like that. Elena is the reason for that smile, and I can't blame my daughter because Elena makes me smile too.

The picture makes me wonder if I've been holding Noah back from feeling joy because I've chosen to live a solitary life.

My eyes drift to Elena's face. Pure and good, she radiates sunshine. She has brought so much into Noah's life in such a short amount of time. For years, I've noticed her across the street. How could I not notice her beauty? But knowing her is so much more than that, so much more than what's on the outside. Between her father and her ex-husband, it's clear she hasn't been treated right. She doesn't know her worth, hasn't been told how incredible she is. The people in her life took her for granted, and that protective part of me flares up, wanting to show her all that she deserves.

Could I? Could I be that man?

My chest aches, and I know what that feeling is.

Longing.

It yearns for someone, something, that I'm not sure I can have. But I want it like hell.

I want *her* like hell.

And the more she entwines herself into my life, the harder it's going to be when she leaves.

And she will leave. I can't see any other outcome.

Elena's headlights flicker through the window, so I head outside.

She hops out of the car and gestures to the passenger side. "She's sleeping."

I duck my head and peer through the window. "She's all partied out, huh?"

"She had a blast. I did too."

"Thank you for taking her. She'll never forget this."

"Will you carry her inside? I feel bad waking her." She glances at Noah and a sweet smile blooms on her face. "Thank you for letting me take her."

The way she looks at my daughter with such affection stirs something inside of me, and I can't stop myself from holding out my hand for her, palm facing the sky.

"Will you dance with me first?"

Her head snaps to me. "What?"

"I'd like to give you that slow dance you missed out on."

Nerves surge through my veins while Elena's eyes flick from my outstretched hand to my eyes.

She could very well reject me. And I'd have to be okay with that.

But then she's climbing the stairs, and her hand is in mine. I settle my left hand on the small of her back, and we shuffle from side to side.

I don't know what the hell I'm doing. My body is stiff and I feel awkward.

This idea worked better in my head.

Elena blinks up at me. "You haven't danced in a while, have you?"

"Is it that obvious?"

She smiles as she takes my right hand and places it with the other on her back. Then she slides her hands around the back of my neck and presses her body against mine.

She blinks up at me as she plays with the hair on the back of my head. "This is better, isn't it?"

"It is."

We're so close, her lavender scent invading my nostrils, her softness pressed against me, her plump lips inches from mine.

Having her in my arms like this feels like too much and not enough all at once.

"I didn't know you were a romantic inside that big ogre heart of yours."

I arch a brow. "Don't tell anyone my secret."

The soft melody of her laughter settles in my bones. She rests her head on my chest, and I hold her in my arms as if she's mine.

As if she could be.

As if I have anything to offer her.

I ROLL over onto my back and stare up at the ceiling.

I've been tossing and turning for the last hour. Maybe I'm just not tired enough yet. Or maybe a certain blonde woman dancing around my head is what's keeping me awake.

I was so close to kissing Elena in the bathroom the other day. I don't know what the hell got into me. But it was clear she wanted me to. Her lips parted, and she looked at me with want and need shining in her eyes. I saw that same look on her tonight as we danced on the porch. She's waiting for me to make a move.

And I don't know what to do with that.

I flick on the lamp and scoot to sit up against my headboard to think.

What would've happened *after* we kissed?

It scares me how excited Noah is to hang out with Elena. Sure, she lives across the street now, but she won't be around forever. Noah is getting attached. And attached means it'll be hard when she needs to detach.

How long would it take Elena to tire of me? Of this lifestyle? She's young and vibrant. She can have anything she wants, do anything she wants. She's not tied down by parenthood. Not that being Noah's father is a prison sentence by any means, but being single in your twenties is a lot different than being a parent in your forties. The novelty of being with a DILF, as she so eloquently put it, would wear off after a while.

A smile tugs at the corners of my mouth just thinking about her nervous rambling. She came into my life the way a tornado does, spawning out of nowhere and throwing everything upside-down. Golden hair, sweet smile, killer curves, and that huge heart. Compassion and love ooze out of her, and you can't not be happy when she's around.

Fuck, I want her. I kick myself and thank the lord that I didn't kiss her, all at the same time.

I've been so worried about Noah getting attached to Elena…yet *I'm* the one getting attached.

My phone buzzes on my nightstand, startling me out of my thoughts.

Elena: What are you doing up?
Me: Are you spying on me?
Elena: I was staring at the moon out my window and I noticed your light on.

Me: I can't sleep. What are you doing up (and looking through my window?)

The phone rings in my hand and I stare down at it like a live bomb. Something about a late-night phone call with Elena feels dangerous. It feels like I'm doing something wrong. It feels…*more*.

Still, I can't help myself as I lift the phone to my ear. "Hi, Elena."

"I wasn't looking through your window. I simply noticed your light was on. You should be thankful to have such a concerned neighbor. There could've been an intruder."

"I don't think an intruder would turn on a light."

"You never know. I was looking out for your safety. And if you happened to walk past the window without a shirt on, then I would've gotten a treat. It's a win-win."

A low laugh escapes me. "Didn't know I was living across the street from a peeping Tom."

"You laughed." She pauses. "I love it when you do that."

I close my eyes and let my head fall back against the headboard. "Maybe I'm not such a mean old ogre anymore."

"You've definitely improved since we became friends."

My stomach sours at the word. "Is that what we are?"

"I think an ogre can be friends with a gnome if he wants to."

"And what if he doesn't want to be friends?"

"That depends what he *does* want."

I whisper the words into the darkness like a shameful confession. "He might just want to eat the little gnome."

Sinful scenes flash through my mind—my head between Elena's thighs, my tongue lapping her up like my favorite dessert, her hands fisting my hair as her hips roll against my face. My dick hardens, waiting for her soft voice to flutter through the phone.

Finally she says, "That's good because she *wants* to be devoured."

Fuck me. She wants this—whatever this is. And right now, in the still of the night, I want it too.

I wrap my hand around my dick and squeeze to give it some kind of relief. "I bet you taste delicious."

"You're welcome to come find out."

What I wouldn't do to give her what she wants, what she needs.

"I wish I could, beautiful."

She hums, and the sound goes straight to my dick. I want to hear all her sounds, her sighs and moans, the way she sounds when she likes what I'm doing to her, the way she sounds when she's getting close to coming, the way she sounds when she's screaming from ecstasy.

The sound of *my* name on her lips.

"Grant?"

"Mhmm?"

"What are you thinking about right now?"

"Things I shouldn't."

She pauses. "Will you do something for me?"

"Sure."

"I want you to touch yourself."

I squeeze my cock again. "I'm already there, babe."

"Me too."

A small moan escapes her, and that sound is my undoing.

I'm consumed by the vision of Elena lying on her bed, legs spread wide, pants around her ankles while she slides her fingers over her pussy. I lose any semblance of control and succumb to the moment.

"Tell me how you like it," I whisper. "Tell me what you're doing."

"I'm rubbing my clit in light teasing circles."

"You like to be teased?"

"Yes." Her voice is breathy and sexy as hell.

I pump my dick in long strokes, envisioning what she's telling me. "I wish I could feel how wet you are."

"You can hear it though." She must move the phone closer because I can hear the slick sound of his fingers moving. "I'm pretending it's you, Grant. I'm pretending my fingers are yours, long and thick." She moans again, louder this time. "I've been fantasizing about you a lot lately."

So honest. "Tell me about one of your fantasies."

"I come over to your house to tutor Noah, but she isn't there. She's at her friend's house. And instead of letting me leave, you invite me to stay for dinner. I help you cook and we're side by side at the counter. Our arms brush and we inch closer, little by little, until we can't stand the tension any longer. Then you grab me by my hips, prop my ass on the counter, and kiss me hard."

I imagine every detail of what she's saying, and I can't deny I've thought about the same exact scenario whenever she's been in my kitchen.

"Then what?" My breaths are ragged as my hand moves up and down my cock.

"You yank down my pants and pull my panties to the side." She's breathing hard, and I squeeze my eyes shut, imagining how fast her fingers are working her pussy right now. "You bite the inside of my thigh before licking your way up between my legs. I hold on to the back of your head and rest my heels on your shoulders, my legs spread wide for you."

"Fuck, Elena."

"Grant, tell me what you'd do to me on your counter."

I pick up right where she left off. "I'd bury my face in your pussy, and tell you how sweet you taste. I'd swirl my tongue over your clit and then drag it all the way back down, gripping on to that incredible ass and pulling you closer so I could suck you into my mouth."

"Oh god."

"I'd reach up and pull down your shirt and your bra so I could play with your nipples, rubbing them and teasing you until you couldn't take it anymore."

She's panting and moaning, and I can tell by her sounds that she's close.

"Come for me, Elena. That's what I'd tell you if you were here right now. I'd beg for you to come on my tongue."

She cries out, and I suppress my groans as I come with her, my dick spilling out onto my bare stomach. Her unrestrained sounds echo in my mind, creating a memory where they'll forever stay.

We wait with each other in silence as our breaths return to normal.

But there's nothing normal about the way my heart is beating in my chest for this woman…long after we say good night and hang up.

13

ELENA

"Hey, Lenny. Over here."

I smile as I make my way over to Val. "Thanks for saving me a seat."

"I had to fight a PTO mom to keep it."

I shake off my jacket and fold it on my lap as I lower myself onto the chair. "Is Jake so excited about his acting debut?"

"He was so nervous, I had to pull over so he could puke before we got here. I think he got some chunks on his turkey costume."

"Oh, no. Poor thing." I clutch my chest. "He's going to be the best turkey this school has ever seen."

Val purses her lips. "Okay, spill the beans. You've been spending a lot of time at Grant's house these last few weeks, and I am dying to know what's going on."

I catch her up to speed on how Grant and I went from enemies to friends, and I leave out the major details about my attraction to him. My head hasn't been on right since he asked me to dance on his porch last weekend, followed by the phone sex. We went from innocent flirting to…I don't even know how to explain what we are.

Val's eyes widen. "Is his daughter as terrible as we thought?"

"No, not at all."

"Really?"

"Really. She's a great kid."

Val nudges me with her shoulder as she waggles her eyebrows. "And Grant? Is he still an asshole?"

I shake my head and give her a rueful look. "No."

"Ah, shit."

"What?"

"You have feelings for him."

"What? No."

She nods. "Yes, you do."

I flick my eyes up to the ceiling and let out a long exhale. "Yes, I do."

"Len, this is a good thing. You're into him. Why do you look like someone died?"

"I'm not ready to acknowledge it because once I do then it's real, and if it's real, then that means I have to figure out what we're doing, and then there's a chance he might not feel the same way, and if he doesn't feel the same way then I'm going to get hurt, and I'm really not ready to get hurt again."

"Whoa. How did you just go from *I like him* to *I'm getting hurt?* Who says you're going to get hurt?"

"This is the first real something I've felt since Neil." I hike a shoulder. "I'm scared."

"Have you told him how you feel?"

"Not in the literal sense." I grimace and lower my voice to a whisper. "We may or may not have had phone sex the other night."

"Phone sex?!" Val's voice screeches, garnering the looks of the nearby parents.

"Oh, my god." I drop my chin to my chest and pray for the floor to swallow me whole. "We're in an elementary school. Keep your voice down."

"Sorry." She holds up her hand and apologizes to the people next to us. "But you can't tell me juicy details like that in an elementary school. How did *that* happen?"

"I don't know. One second, we were talking, and the next thing I know…" Heat rushes into my cheeks. "It just happened."

"He's clearly attracted to you. You don't have phone calls like that unless you're into someone. And you're both single. You're both attracted to each other, so there's nothing standing between you. This sounds perfect to me."

I hike a shoulder. "I don't know how he feels about me. Or about relationships. He's been single for a long time. Maybe he doesn't want something serious."

"Come on, Len. You're amazing. Of course he's going to fall madly in love with you and want to be with you forever."

I chuckle. "You sound so confident about that."

"It's the truth."

"When I'm with him, it feels like he likes me. But when I'm not with him, I convince myself that it's nothing. He hasn't come out and said anything about being with me."

"Only one way to find out. You have to talk to him."

Talk. That isn't Grant's favorite pastime.

"Damn. Ms. Canterbury is going to be heartbroken. She has a thing for him."

My chin jerks back. "The old lady with seven cats who lives down the block?"

Val nods, biting the inside of her cheek to keep from laughing. "I think she's a closet freak."

"I did not need to know that." But I laugh imagining what Grant's reaction will be when I tell him. "I can't wait to tell him that. It's so fun to fuck with him."

"And even more fun when you literally do fuck him."

Several people sitting in the row in front of us turn around and give us disgusted looks.

I cover my face with my hands. "We're done with this conversation."

"Oh, look. The PTO mom is looking over here to see if I was lying about saving the seat for you. Wave to the nice psycho lady."

I giggle as I wave to the red-haired lady who's glaring at us.

The curtain rises, and a hush falls over the room as the show begins.

And for the next thirty minutes, I tell myself that I'm just a woman who's here to see her friend's kid perform instead of a woman who will never get to sit in a school to watch her *own* kid perform.

When I pull up to my house, Grant's truck catches my eye in his driveway.

That's odd. He's home early. I shoot him a text to make sure everything is okay.

Me: Are you playing hooky or are you sick?
Grant: My back went out.
Me: Oh no. Are you okay? Do you need anything?
Grant: Wait, why are you home?
Me: I took the day off to see my friend's son in his school play.
Grant: I could actually use some help. I don't want Noah to come home and see me on the floor.
Me: You're on the floor?!
Grant: Do NOT make a Life Alert joke right now.
Grant: There's a spare key under the mat by the front door.

I jog across the street and let myself into Grant's house.

"I'm here." My eyes dart around the living room and kitchen. "Where are you?"

His voice comes from upstairs. "My bedroom."

I take the stairs by twos. If his house is like mine, then his bedroom should be to the left. I stick my head through the doorway and spot Grant lying on his stomach on the floor at the foot of his bed with Romeo lying next to him.

I rush over to him and kneel down. "What happened?"

"I dropped off Noah at school and then I came home to get ready for work." He lets out a long breath and rolls his eyes. "I bent down to tie my boots and I must've twisted the wrong way. This happens to me from time to time."

"Have you seen a doctor?"

"No."

"Grant."

"Can you at least help me up before you yell at me?"

"Who said anything about helping you up?" I scratch Romeo's head and he licks my arm. "You did a good job staying here with Daddy."

"Sure, you're nice to him," Grant mutters.

"If you make an appointment with an orthopedist, I'll rub your belly. How does that sound?"

He grunts. "I just might like that."

I push off the floor and stand. "All right. Let's get you to the bed."

"I need to take my time. Just hold my arm, and don't let me fall."

"Sounds easy enough." I bend forward and hold out my arms, hooking one under his shoulder. "Come on, you big ogre. Nice and easy."

Grant slowly rolls onto his side and winces as he moves to a seated position. I let him take his time, my heart aching at the sight of how much pain he's in.

"On three."

I nod and plant my feet shoulder-width apart. "One…two…"

"Three." Grant braces himself with his left hand on the edge of his bed and hoists himself up while I support him on the right as he stands.

But he's not steady on his feet. His legs wobble as he hisses in pain and teeters to one side.

"Grant…"

He leans his weight on me. "Fuck."

I struggle to hold him as he fights for balance, my knees buckling. If I don't think of something fast, we'll both be on the floor. I muster all my strength and shove him toward the bed instead. He falls back onto the mattress and pulls me down with him. I land on top of him, chest to chest.

"Shit." I brace my hands on either side of him, propping myself up to avoid hurting him even more. "I lost my balance, and I figured the bed would be a better landing place than the floor."

"You're right." He blinks up at me, his dark eyes searching my face. "This is better."

My skin heats. "I mean, I'm not opposed to the view I had when I walked in either."

His eyebrow tics. "Were you checking out my ass?"

"Kind of hard not to."

He skims his hands down my spine and settles on my lower back. "I know what you mean."

If he weren't hurt, I'd mount him right here and beg him to rip off my clothes. The memory of our phone sex replays through my mind.

But he's in pain, and I need to keep my mind out of the gutter, so I carefully start to climb off him.

Grant grips my waist. "Don't."

I freeze, hovering over him.

"What were you just thinking about?"

My cheeks burn with embarrassment or desire, I can't be sure. "Nothing."

He lifts his hand to my cheek and his thumb brushes over my lips. "Tell me, Elena."

A shiver of need dances down my spine and my stomach clenches. "I was wishing that you weren't in pain because I want to straddle you."

"Straddle me."

Those two words have wetness pooling between my legs. "But I don't want to hurt you."

"The pain is nothing compared to the way I'd feel if you got up and left right now."

Excitement rushes through my veins.

I swing my leg over him and plant my knees on either side of his hips. Then I take his hands and guide them down onto my ass. "This is what I was thinking about."

He squeezes two handfuls. "Fuck, your body is perfect."

I widen my legs and lower myself onto the hardness bulging out of his sweatpants, rolling my hips once to see if it hurts him.

"Mmm." His gaze falls to my mouth. "I should pull my back out more often."

I roll my hips again, relishing in the feel of him through my yoga pants. "Imagine what you could do to me if you weren't in pain."

He smirks. "I'll make an appointment with the doctor tomorrow."

"Good boy."

I run my hands along his chest, feeling the hard muscle under his thin T-shirt as I roll my hips once more. His fingers dig into my ass, squeezing me hard. Then I lean down, bringing my lips closer to his. I hover over his mouth, counting the seconds as I wait for him to stop me.

But he doesn't.

I press my lips to his, the light contact sending electric sparks throughout my entire body. I do it again and again, rocking my hips in sync with our mouths. He keeps one hand on my ass and moves the other up my back, settling between my shoulder blades, holding me against him.

I slip my tongue between his lips, and he opens in an instant, his tongue winding around mine to deepen our kiss. I moan into his mouth and our pace picks up as I shamelessly chase a release. He grips the hair at the base of my neck, fisting it in his hand.

The room fills with the sound of our panting. Grant slides his hand under my shirt, and I reach behind my back and unclasp my bra, giving him access to what he wants. Both of his large hands push up my bra and cup my breasts as he lets out a loud groan. He plays with my nipples, swirling his thumbs over the hardened buds. He cranes his neck and takes one into his mouth, grunting like he's feasting on me. I arch my back and push my chest against him, relishing in the feel of his warm tongue on me. Burning pleasure mounts between my legs as I rub myself against his dick.

"Are you wet, Elena?" His deep voice rasps against my skin.

I take one of his hands and guide him to the edge of my waistband. "See for yourself."

His eyes lock with mine as he slips his fingers under my panties. "Fuck, you're soaked for me."

I ride his fingers, moaning his name in his ear. "Grant, you feel so good."

"You're going to come all over my hand." He slips a finger inside me while his thumb plays with my clit. "I want to watch how beautiful you look when you come and then I want to taste you dripping from my fingers."

Oh god. His words spur me on. I reach down into his boxers and wrap my hand around him, jerking him in hard strokes. I break our kiss to look down between us. He's long and thick, matching every other part of him, and my pussy clenches at the thought of taking him inside me.

"You're going to make me come way too soon if you keep looking at my dick like that."

I run my thumb over his swollen crown before dragging my hand back down and squeezing him at the base of his cock. "Good, because I want you to come with me, and I'm close."

He curls another finger inside me, and I see stars.

We're panting into each other's mouths, grunting and moaning, hands and hips frantic like wild animals, until I clench around his fingers, white-hot ecstasy shooting through me like a firework.

Grant comes with me. The intensity in his gaze takes my breath away, and I keep my eyes locked on him, watching the raw vulnerability slip through his armor as he calls my name like a prayer. This big, beautiful man succumbs to me like he's powerless under my touch.

His eyes won't release me after we're both sated, not even as he brings his fingers to his mouth and hums his approval. "Fucking delicious."

Heat creeps into my cheeks, and I glance down at my disheveled appearance—bra undone, shirt pushed up under my chin, pants twisted.

I can't believe that just happened.

But goddamn, *was that hot.*

"I didn't hurt you at all, did I?"

He lets out a raspy chuckle. "Not even close."

"Are you sure? Because you're injured, and I just jumped on top of you and humped you like a dog in heat."

Romeo lifts his head from his bed in the corner of the room, his collar jingling from the motion.

Grant pulls me down and kisses my lips. "I loved every second of it."

So did I.

After I clean up the mess he made on his stomach, I get him settled into a comfortable position in bed and place a heating pad on his back.

"Is there anything else I can do?"

Grant clasps my hand. "Will you lay with me?"

My heart thumps a furious rhythm against my chest. "Of course."

I snuggle into his king-size bed, surrounded by his familiar scent. His eyelids droop closed, but before he falls asleep, he wraps his arm around me and pulls me close.

"You're beautiful, Elena."

I press my lips to his temple and whisper. "So are you."

I watch him as he drifts to sleep and commit every second of this moment to memory.

Almost as if there's something deep inside of me that knows this won't last.

Grant

"Put your two fingers down like this and keep your index finger and your pinkie up."

Noah wiggles her thumb. "What do I do with this one?"

"You can keep it up or tuck it down with the others. I like

keeping it up."

Noah thrusts her rock-and-roll hands in the air and shouts, "Rock on, baby!"

I stifle a laugh so they don't know I'm here. I've been watching them in the kitchen for the last ten minutes from behind the wall.

I woke up to an empty bed and panicked when I realized what time it was. My back spasms calmed down, so I was able to hobble downstairs. But when I saw Elena and Noah cooking together in the kitchen, I couldn't bring myself to alert them of my presence.

Metallica plays from Elena's phone. She bangs on a set of imaginary drums while Noah pretends to play the guitar in between chopping vegetables and tossing them into a pot on the stove.

"What kind of music does your dad listen to?" Elena asks.

"He doesn't really listen to anything."

Elena snorts. "No wonder he's so grumpy all the time."

Smartass.

"He hasn't been so grumpy lately." Noah side-eyes Elena before she continues. "He's nicer when you're around."

"You think so?"

Noah nods. "He likes when you're around. I can tell."

I catch the smile that blooms on Elena's face before she bites the inside of her cheek to hide it.

Yeah, I like when she's around. More than I'd like to admit.

And after what we did this afternoon? *Fuck me.* I don't know how to act around her now because all I want to do is pull her close and kiss her.

"I like it when you're around too," Noah adds.

Elena sets the knife on the counter and turns to face Noah. "I like being around you, kid."

"It feels nice having another girl around the house." Noah shrugs. "It feels like I'm not so alone."

Alone? Why hasn't she told me she feels alone? And why does she feel alone when she has me?

"You are never alone. Your father loves you more than life itself, and you always have me." Elena stops the music on her phone. "What's going on? Did something happen?"

Noah picks at her fingernail. "Hannah got her period yesterday."

"Ah." Elena nods like she understands something I don't. "And you haven't gotten yours yet?"

She shakes her head. "I've been worried about it because I don't have a mom to go to. Hannah was with her mom all day, and she told me the things she said and…"

"And your dad won't be able to have that conversation with you."

Noah wipes her nose with the back of her hand. "Certain things are just awkward with him."

"That's normal. I wouldn't have wanted to talk about my dad with any of those things either." Elena cups Noah's face. "Would you like to talk about it with me?"

Noah nods. "You would do that?"

"Of course I will." Elena grabs Noah's shoulders and pulls her into a hug. "Lord knows your dad can't handle hearing about tampons and ovaries."

A laugh bursts from Noah's throat and she hugs Elena harder.

Tightness in my chest makes it hard to suck in my next breath. Watching them together like this, something settles deep in my bones. It's more than the fact that Elena is good with kids. More than the fact that she's hot as hell and made me come in my pants like a teenager.

It's more than anything I've ever felt.

Watching someone love your child makes your heart crack wide open. Elena doesn't have to love Noah. She doesn't have to help her or be there for her. Noah's own mother relinquished those rights. But Elena is here, day in and day out, choosing to be here for my daughter without getting anything in return.

It's special.

It means something.

For over a decade, Noah has been all I've needed.

But for the first time, I've found something that I want.

I just don't know if I can have both.

14

GRANT

"Are you okay, Dad?"

I glare at my daughter. "I'm fine. Why do you two keep asking me if I'm okay?"

"Your eye twitches every time we put an ornament on the tree." Noah places a red ball way too close to a green one. "See? It happened again."

I slap my palm over my twitchy eye. "I'm just tired. Someone in this room woke me up at the ass-crack of dawn."

Romeo whimpers and lowers his head, not making eye contact with me.

"He can't help it." Elena scratches behind his ears. "He was excited to decorate for Christmas."

"And *I* was excited to sleep in on my day off."

"There's Christmas music playing." Noah plants her hand on her hip. "You can't be grumpy when there's Christmas music."

I cross my arms over my chest. "That's exactly why I'm grumpy."

Elena's eyes widen. "You don't like Christmas music?"

I almost laugh. She looks horrified as if I just told her that I worship Satan.

"The Grinch is more his style." Noah sifts through the tub we took down from the attic. "There's a Grinch ornament in here somewhere."

Elena saunters over to me and bounces onto the couch beside me. "The Grinch's heart grows at the end of the movie, you know."

I smirk. "All because of a pesky little blonde."

She jabs me in my ribs. "Are you calling me pesky?"

I resist the urge to grip her hips and pull her on top of me. "Never."

She gives me a playful roll of her eyes. "Mhmm."

"How was Thanksgiving with your mother yesterday?"

"She has her good days and bad days, and sometimes she doesn't recognize me." Elena picks at a thread sticking out of her sweater. "Yesterday was a good day. I enjoyed spending the time with her."

I squeeze her knee. "Maybe Noah and I can come with you one day."

Her eyebrows perk up. "Really?"

"I've been reading about Alzheimer's and it said that visitors can cheer them up and keep them occupied."

Elena blinks. "You've been reading about it?"

I nod. "I have."

She covers my hand with hers, staring at me with wide eyes like she's in disbelief. "That's really…sweet."

I suppose I can't blame her for being surprised. I've been taking myself by surprise lately too. Instead of pushing Elena away, I keep opening myself up and letting her in further. I don't know what I'm doing, but I know that I can't seem to help myself where she's concerned.

"Noah saved you a slice of my mother's pie." I glance over at her on the floor. "Did you find the tree topper in there yet?"

"No, but I found this." Noah stares down at a small white envelope.

My stomach churns as I slide off the couch and onto the floor beside her. "Those are your mother's pictures."

Elena lowers herself onto the carpet and slips her hand into mine, and I'm suddenly aware of how happy I am that she's here for this. I always imagined I'd go through this alone, worried that I wouldn't know what to say. But with Elena by our sides, I know she'll help make everything okay for Noah.

Noah hesitates. "I've always wondered what she looked like."

I smooth my palm against her back in small circles. "Open it."

There aren't many pictures in there, but I asked Tara's parents for pictures from various stages of her life. I wanted Noah to be able to see what her mother looked like as a baby, as a teen, and as an adult.

Noah pulls out the photos and lifts the first one close to her face. "Oh, wow."

Elena leans over her shoulder. "She was beautiful."

Noah looks like me, but the shape of her nose and the dimples in her cheeks are unmistakably from her mother.

"She looked happy here." Noah's eyes meet mine. "How could she look this happy when she was so troubled?"

I hike a shoulder. "She had her ups and downs."

She flips through the pictures and blinks past the welling tears. "I wonder if she would've gotten better if she didn't die."

Her words pierce my heart like a bullet. "She was sick. I don't think there was anything anyone could've done to help her."

She wipes a tear as it falls. "I hate that I never got to know her before she died."

My eyebrows pop. "But you would've been devastated when you lost her."

"At least I would've known her, even if it was for a little while."

How could she think that? It's better to not know what you lost than to have to live with the memories. Bile rises in my throat, but I swallow it down. Now isn't the time to try to convince Noah that it's better this way. She needs me to be here for her, and hear her.

Elena reaches out and squeezes her shoulder. "She couldn't see what she was missing. Your dad is right. She was sick, and she wasn't in her right mind. Otherwise, she would've fought to stay for you."

Noah sniffles. "Can I keep these in my room?"

I'd prefer them in the attic, but it's not about what I want. Not with this.

"We can get a nice frame to put them in, if you'd like."

Her eyes widen. "Really? You'd let me do that?"

I hate how shocked she is that I'd let her put a picture in a frame. Have I really been so controlling over every aspect of her life?

"Yes, of course."

Noah wraps her arms around me and hugs me tight. "Thank you. This means a lot to me, Dad."

I hold her in my arms—my whole world—and hope she can feel how much I love her. How every decision I've ever made has been for her.

Noah turns her attention back to the tree, and Elena excuses herself to the bathroom.

I wait in the hall for her to come back out.

She clutches her chest when she swings open the door. "Jesus, you scared me."

"I'm sorry." I pull her close and stroke her cheek with my thumb. "Just wanted to make sure you were okay. I saw you getting a little emotional back there."

"I'm really proud of you, Grant."

My eyebrows lift. "Me? What did I do?"

"You didn't tell Noah how she *should* feel. You heard her. And you agreed to let her keep the pictures in her room." Elena shakes her head. "That meant a lot to her, and you gave it to her."

I graze the tip of my nose against hers. "You're teaching me how to be a better listener."

She pulls me back into the bathroom and presses her lips to mine.

I slide my hand into her hair, cradling the back of her head as I deepen the kiss and sweep my tongue inside her mouth. Heat rushes through my veins like it always does whenever I touch this woman.

She lets out a quiet moan as she fists my shirt in her hands, and the vibration of that sound goes straight to my dick.

Noah's voice interrupts our moment as she yells from the living room. "I found the tree topper!"

I rest my forehead against Elena's.

"I'll go out first," she whispers. "You can calm down that situation in your pants."

Elena

"Ms. Donaldson, please have a seat."

I lower myself into the chair opposing my lawyer's desk. "Thank you for fitting me into your busy schedule."

"Of course. I was surprised to hear about what's been going on." She flips open her notepad. "Tell me more about it."

I let out a long breath as I wring my hands in my lap. "Neil has been pressuring me to sell the house so he can have his half of it."

"Pressuring you how?"

"He started by calling and texting me. A lot. Then he showed up at the house last month."

Her pen pauses on the paper as her eyes flick to mine. "And what did he say when he came to your house?"

"That he wants me to sell because he's entitled to half of it. He also said the house is too big for me. But his fiancée is pregnant, and I know they could use the money, so that's the real reason he's hounding me."

"I'm glad you came to me. Neil shouldn't be harassing you to sell the house. You both agreed to the terms of your divorce." Annalise sets down her pen and leans back in her chair. "Send me the phone log so we have evidence of his texts and calls. Do you have any proof that he came to your house that day?"

I nod. "I have footage from the Ring camera."

"Good. Email me everything, and I'll contact his lawyer to let him know that if this behavior continues, he'll be in violation of his divorce agreement."

"My friend said I should file a restraining order against him, but I don't think that's necessary. Neil wouldn't do anything to physically harm me."

She shrugs. "Anyone is capable of anything when money is on the line."

I rub my forehead. "Sometimes I think that I should move to a smaller house and give him the money so he leaves me alone."

"You didn't agree to give him half the house *when* you sell. You agreed to give him half if you sell. He shouldn't be persuading you to sell, nor should he be talking to you at all. We'll put a stop to this."

I hope so.

After our meeting, I head home.

But when I pull into the driveway, my heart stutters.

Grant and Noah are sitting on my porch with a beautiful bouquet of flowers in Noah's hands.

I fling open my door. "What's going on?"

Noah stands and holds out the bouquet in front of her. "We thought you might be upset after speaking with the lawyer, so Dad wanted to be here for you to cheer you up."

My eyes find Grant's as he rises from the steps and shoves his hands in his pockets, a small smirk tugging at the corner of his mouth.

"This is so thoughtful." I walk toward the porch and take the flowers from Noah, pulling her into a hug. "Thank you."

"You're welcome." She pulls back and tugs my hand. "Come on. Dad is going to cook in your kitchen tonight because this is your house."

I smile. "I love that idea."

As we head inside, Grant nudges me with his shoulder. "How did it go?"

"She's going to contact Neil's lawyer. I have to send her the calls and texts, as well as the footage from the surveillance camera."

"Guess that creepy camera came in handy, huh?"

I chuckle. "Yes, it did. You're right every once in a while."

"I'm just glad you told your lawyer what he's been doing." Grant stops and lets Noah go ahead of us into the kitchen. "You deserve to stay in this house for as long as you want to."

"I wouldn't want to move now anyway. I kind of like being across the street from you guys."

"You should just move in with us," Noah calls from the other room, clearly able to hear everything we're saying.

I bite my lip to keep from smiling. It's sweet that Noah wants that to happen, but it's way too soon to move in with each other.

Only Grant doesn't tell Noah that. He presses his lips against my forehead and follows her into the kitchen.

15

GRANT

"Full house, bitches."

We all groan and toss our cards onto the table.

Mitch cackles as he sweeps the pile of chips over to his side of the table. "Don't hate the player, hate the game."

Jason scrubs his hand over his face. "Dude, no one says that anymore."

Mitch shrugs. "What's the lingo now? What are the kids saying these days?"

I point a finger at Jason. "Do not give him any new slang to butcher. I'm still mad at Noah for teaching him the word *bussin'*."

Trent chuckles. "Where is Noah tonight? I was looking forward to watching her school her old man in poker."

"She's at the neighbor's house across the street." I glance at my phone. "She should be back soon."

The neighbor's house sounds easier than anything else. I don't know what to call Elena, and anything more would raise suspicion among the guys. I haven't told them about her because I'm not sure what exactly to say.

As if my thoughts conjured her, the sound of the front door opening has me on my feet.

"There she is." Trent stands and opens his arms wide as Noah runs into the dining room and slams into him. "I was just asking about you."

"I was baking cookies at Lenny's house." She pulls away and gestures to the hallway. "Len, come in and meet my dad's friends."

Panic clenches my stomach in a vise grip.

Here the fuck we go.

Elena comes into the room with tentative steps and her eyes immediately find mine, like she isn't sure if she should be here. "Hey, everyone."

All three of my friends stare at her as if she's a seven-foot alien from *Avatar*, eyes wide and mouths agape.

"She lives across the street," Noah explains. "Lenny, this is Trent, Mitch, and Jason."

"It's nice to meet you." She offers a small wave. "Sorry for intruding on boys' night, but we baked cookies." She holds up a plate covered in plastic wrap.

"Not an intrusion at all." Mitch is quick to pull out the chair beside him. "Stay a while. We were hoping to watch Noah kick her father's ass in a few rounds of poker."

Her eyes flick to mine again. "Thank you for the offer, but I should get going. Maybe another time."

"Ah, come on." Trent lowers himself back into his seat and reaches for the deck. "We'll deal you in. Do you know how to play poker?"

She nods. "I have an idea."

Mitch blinks at me. "Come on, Grant. Tell the lady she's more than welcome to stay."

I swallow. "Of course, you're welcome to stay if you want to."

Jason lifts a bowl of chips. "I've got Doritos if you come sit next to me."

Mitch scoffs. "I already pulled out the chair for her. Young boys like you don't know how to romance a lady."

Jason tosses a chip at him. "You wouldn't know what to do with a lady if she came over and sat on your face."

Noah's top lip curls. "Eww."

I reach over and smack Jason in the back of the head. "Hey, not in front of my kid."

With red cheeks, Elena eyes the only two empty seats at the table and takes the one beside Noah, which just so happens to be the one on the other side of Jason.

And Jason grins like the cat that ate the canary.

Smug bastard.

"I think I remember how to play." Elena collects her cards and glances at them. "You want to make a straight or a flush, right?"

"Pairs are good too." Jason moves his chair way too close to hers, as if he needs to physically spot her in order to play.

Watch your hands, fucker.

I get dealt a shit hand and fold, or maybe it's a perfectly good hand. I don't know. I can't concentrate with the way Jason is looking at Elena like a kid on Christmas morning.

It comes down to Noah, Mitch, and Elena.

"All right, Noah. I think you're bluffing." Mitch flips over his cards. "Let me see what you've got."

Noah grins as she tosses her cards onto the table. "Straight."

Mitch balks. "How do you always beat me? I can never tell if you're bluffing."

"Because I'm just that good." Noah flips her hair over her shoulder, then glances across the table. "Whatcha got, Lenny?"

Elena's lips tug into the smallest smirk. "Are these any good?"

We watch as she flips over a four and a six, both hearts.

Noah gasps. "You have a straight flush."

She shrugs, feigning innocence. "Maybe it's just beginner's luck."

Trent shakes his head. "Beginner's luck, my ass. I call bullshit."

Elena's smirk breaks into a full-blown grin. "I used to play with my grandparents all the time growing up."

Mitch claps. "She's gonna give you a run for your money, Noah."

Noah laughs. "That was awesome. I totally didn't see that coming."

Jason high-fives Elena, and something twinges in my chest as I watch them laugh together. It's like I'm on the outside looking in. They look good together—a happy young couple.

And reality crashes down on me like a ton of bricks.

What an idiot I've been.

All this time, I've been deluding myself into thinking we could actually be together. But Jason is the kind of person she belongs with. They make sense.

I'm in no position to be with a young woman like her. My life isn't over, but it's set. I'm stationary. Settled. Elena is at the edge of what her life is about to become. She'll get remarried and want to have kids someday. I can't give her that life. She needs to be with someone who can give her everything she wants—and I have no right stopping her.

My lungs constrict, like the room is caving in on me, and I can't breathe.

"Dad, are you okay?" Noah gestures to my hand that's rubbing the spot under my collarbone.

My eyes snap to Noah and my hand drops from the burning in my chest. "Yeah, I'm fine. Just some indigestion."

Jason collects the chips. "Okay, shark. Double or nothing."

I fold the next three rounds, unable to focus on anything aside from the racing thoughts bouncing off the walls of my head.

"I'm out, guys." Elena tosses her cards onto the table. "I think I'm going to call it a night."

Noah whines. "Come on, Len. Will you please stay?"

Jason leans toward her. "Yeah, come on, Len. Stay a little longer."

Before she can answer, I push out of my chair. "She said she's leaving. Say good night, Noah."

Trent arches a brow, and Mitch tilts his head, but I ignore them.

"Good night, everyone." Elena waves around the table. "It was nice meeting you."

She hugs Noah, and then I lead Elena to the front door.

She looks up at me with tentative eyes. "I didn't mean to crash your boys' night."

Guilt squeezes my chest. "It's fine."

She reaches out and rubs my shoulder. "Are you okay?"

"Yeah, just tired. It's been a long day."

"Well, I'll be up reading for a while in bed." Her lips twist into a smirk. "You know, in case you can't sleep later."

My dick twitches at her suggestion in spite of myself. "Good night, Elena."

She reaches up onto her toes and presses her lips to my cheek—and I just stand here like a moron.

I watch her until she's safe inside her house before returning to the dining room.

Three pairs of eyes land on me.

Mitch starts with me right away. "You have some explaining to do, my friend. Who is that beautiful woman, and why have you been hiding her from us?"

My eyes dart around the table. "Where's Noah?"

"She went upstairs to call her friend." Trent kicks out my chair. "Have a seat. Let's chat."

"She looks young." Jason folds his arms over his chest. "How old is she?"

I grab two empty beer bottles from the table and move toward the kitchen. "I think it's time for you guys to get going."

Trent howls as he shoots up out of his seat. "Oh, no. You can't introduce us to a woman like that and not give us an explanation."

"She's just the neighbor," I call over my shoulder as I head into the kitchen, knowing damn well that Elena is way more than just the neighbor.

"'*Just the neighbor*' he says." Mitch chuckles, following me inside. "You have eyeballs. I know you see what she looks like."

I spin around. "And what do her looks have to do with anything, hmm? What are you insinuating?"

Trent puts his hands on his waist. "She's too old to be one of Noah's friends, and you haven't even so much as spoken about a woman in years, let alone allow her to hang out with your daughter. We're just…curious."

"She's been helping Noah with her math. That's it."

The lie tastes like acid on my tongue because that is so not it.

Jason enters the room and leans against the counter. "So then you wouldn't mind if I asked for her number?"

I swallow down the ball of anger in my throat. "I don't think she'd appreciate it if I just gave out her number like that."

He shoves his hands into his pockets. "I could go ring her bell and ask for it."

The thought of Jason anywhere near Elena makes me want to rip off his head and punt it.

But I can't be selfish. I can't claim her for myself.

My hands clench and unclench, torn with what to say. "Be my guest, Jay. She's in the white house across the street."

Mitch shakes his head. "Fucking disappointing."

"What is?"

"You, man. You're clearly into her, but you won't let yourself admit it."

I brace my hands on the counter and squeeze my eyes shut.

Just tell them.

"Is she into you?" Jason asks.

"I don't know."

"You think she's baking cookies with your daughter on a Friday night because she isn't into you?" Mitch laughs. "She getting paid?"

I shoot him a glare. "No."

"Exactly."

"Hey, this is a good thing." Trent rests his hand on my shoulder. "Don't you think it'd be good for Noah to finally see her father in a healthy, happy relationship? How is she going to know what to base her own love life on if you don't show her?"

I swallow past the lump lodged in my throat. "I was hoping she'd base it off the love I show her."

"She needs more than that." Trent squeezes my shoulder. "You need more."

"Look at me and Janelle," Mitch says. "She is ten years younger than me, and we worked out just fine."

"That's because you met her when she was thirty-eight. Elena is in her twenties." I rake my fingers through my hair. "Her fucking twenties. Do you remember what life was like then?"

"What was *your* life like when you were in your twenties, hmm?" Trent levels me with a look. "Weren't you the one raising a baby?"

"Yeah, and look at the stupid decisions I made back then." I lower my voice. "I was an idiot who got his one-night stand pregnant and changed my life forever. I was forced to grow up. I can't ask Elena to do that."

"But Noah isn't a baby anymore. Look at her." Trent gestures upstairs. "Elena clearly likes spending time with her, otherwise she wouldn't spend her Friday night baking cookies with *the neighbor's kid.*"

"And what happens when she wants kids of her own?"

The room falls silent.

I let out a sardonic laugh. "I can't raise another baby. I'm in a different stage of life. What's the point in getting involved with her when she'll want to have kids, and I can't give that to her?"

"Does she want kids?" Jason asks.

I shrug. "If she doesn't now, she will later on. And I won't be the one to stop her from having everything she wants."

"You didn't even ask her? You always do that." Trent shakes his head. "You assume what's best for everyone without talking to them, or giving them a chance."

"Your life isn't over, man." Mitch reaches into his pocket and pulls out his car keys. "I'd hate to see you realize that when it's too late."

"My life isn't over, but hers is just beginning. We're in two different places." I shake my head. "It won't work. And that's the end of it."

Trent claps me on the back. "You should talk to her."

Jason lingers in the kitchen as the guys shuffle into the hallway. "You're not going to talk to her, are you?"

I let out a long sigh. "There's nothing to say. You should go to her house. You'd be great together."

"And how will you feel if she chooses me?"

Can't feel bad when you expect it.

Right?

16

ELENA

"What are you going to do?"

"I don't know." I grimace and turn the phone so Simone can see where I am. "I'm parked down the block. I'm not ready to go home yet."

"Lenny, you have to face him at some point. You can't avoid this forever."

As if Grant knows we're talking about him, a text pops up on the screen.

Grant: How are you feeling today?

I stifle a groan. "He just asked how I'm feeling. I have to tutor Noah."

"Go over there and talk to him. You can't keep pretending you have a headache."

"What am I going to say? *Why did you send Jason over to my house to get my number when I thought you liked me?*' That sounds so stupid."

"That sounds like the truth. Guys are idiots, Len. You have to spell everything out for them. Grant probably has no idea that you're into him."

I squeeze my eyes shut and rest my head on the steering wheel. "How could he not know? I literally dry humped him on his bed."

Simone sighs. "Look, I'm your best friend, and I know you better than anyone else. I know what's going to happen. You're waiting until you don't feel upset anymore, and then you're going to let it blow over and not tell him anything. But the pain is still sitting there inside of you. It doesn't just disappear. You have to tell him how you feel, regardless of how he feels. It's not about him. It's about you speaking your truth."

A frown tugs at my lips. "I hate when you call me out on my shit."

When Jason showed up at my door on Friday night, I politely told him that I wasn't interested and said goodnight. But I was angry. I wanted to march over to Grant's house and yell at him for sending his friend over to my house like that. Instead, I've been avoiding him like a coward for the last couple of days.

But avoiding him means avoiding Noah, and I won't keep doing that to her.

"You're afraid to put yourself out on a limb because you don't want to get knocked off it. But love is all about taking chances. The scarier it is, the more important it is. So, speak your truth. Follow your heart. And any other Pinterest quotes you need—pretend I said them."

I sit back and let my head fall against the headrest. "You're right."

"I know I am. Go home, and call me later and let me know what happens."

I hang up, and before I pull up to my house, I shoot Grant a quick text.

Me: Better. Be there in 5.

. . .

I RUN inside my house to change into something comfortable. Then I jog across the street and ring his doorbell.

Grant swings open the door and my heart leaps into my throat at the sight of him in a white T-shirt with those damn gray sweatpants. It's only been four days, but it feels like longer.

"Hey."

I slip my hands into my coat pockets to keep them from reaching out for him. "Hey. Can you come outside for a minute? I need to talk to you, and I don't want Noah to hear."

"Sure." He steps onto the porch and closes the door behind him. "Is everything okay?"

My nervous stomach ties itself into a knot. "No, actually. I'm mad at you."

His eyebrows jump. "What did I do?"

My hands ball into fists, and I fight to keep my breathing even. *Don't word-vomit. Don't word-vomit.*

"Your friend Jason came to my house the other night. He asked for my number."

Grant folds his arms across his chest. "I know."

"He said you told him it was okay."

He nods. "I did."

He's so calm and collected, unaffected as if he doesn't care one bit.

How could he not care? Has everything between us been one-sided? Am I the only one who feels something between us?

My anger rises like a mounting wave. "I told him I wasn't interested."

His head tilts. "Why not?"

"Why not?" I let out a maniacal laugh. "Because I'm interested in *you*, you idiot!"

Grant's arms fall to his sides as he blinks and says nothing.

"Where is the man who slammed Neil against his car for making me trip? That man wouldn't have let one of his friends make a move on me." I step into his space and jab his chest with my index finger. "You slow danced with me on your porch." I poke his chest again. "You told me I'm beautiful." Another poke. "You kissed me, and we shared an intimate moment together—and I don't do that with just anybody, by the way." I plant my hands on my hips. "I thought it was more than that. I thought you liked me, Grant. And when Jason came to my door, I felt stupid because if you liked me, then you wouldn't have sent someone over to my house to hit on me. But I guess I'm the only one who's feeling something here, and that makes me feel stupid too."

I swallow past the lump in my throat. "So, I pretended to have a headache these last few days because I'm mad at you, and apparently when I'm mad at people, I isolate myself until the anger dies down, and then I don't bother to say anything. But I'm here right now saying something, feeling really vulnerable, because maybe there's a chance you do like me. Maybe I'm not crazy. Maybe I didn't misread all the signals. Maybe you're just too scared to make a move, so here I am making one."

He lifts his hand to rub the back of his neck. "I figured you'd go for a guy like Jason. He's a good kid, and he's around your age."

My head jerks back. "What does his age have to do with anything?"

"You're thirteen years younger than me, Elena. You belong with someone like him. You can get married and have a family of your own." He clenches his jaw and gestures to himself. "You don't want this."

A family of my own.

Tears sting the backs of my eyes.

Don't cry, Len. Stay strong.

"You don't get to tell me what I want or who I belong with. That's not your call to make. Just because you're older doesn't mean you know better—clearly, because you're thirteen years older than me, yet your head is still up your ass." I bite my bottom lip to keep it from trembling. "I know it's been a while since you've had a woman around, and I know you're used to your simple life with Noah. But I was hoping...I guess I was hoping you'd be able to make a little room for me. I love that kid, and I'd never do anything to hurt her. Even if you and I stopped talking for whatever reason, I'd still be there for her. You don't have to worry about that, if that's what's holding you back."

"I *always* have to worry about that." His voice rises. "Noah is all I worry about. Night and day, it's her. I don't have time to waste with someone who will turn around in a year or two and leave because I can't give her the things she wants."

"You didn't even ask me what I want." I reach out and clasp his hand. "Because if you did, I'd tell you that I want you. You and Noah. Package deal. We can take things slow, whatever you need. You can't let fear get in the way of your heart."

He looks down at our laced fingers with his jaw set and his eyebrows pinched.

He's overthinking this like he does with everything. He's trying to make logic out of emotion.

Come on, big guy. Give me something here.

But he pulls back his hand. "You don't understand because you don't have kids of your own, but you will one day, and it'll all make sense to you. You'll understand why I'm doing this."

He might as well have pulled a dagger out and stabbed me with it. I actually think it would've hurt less than the words he chose.

A lone tear slips out and rolls down my cheek. I can barely form the words because it feels as if all the air has been sucked out of my lungs. "I'll never be able to have kids of my own. But you wouldn't know that because you haven't bothered to have a conversation with me about it."

His eyes narrow. "What?"

"Doesn't matter though, does it? You'll just keep coming up with reasons why we shouldn't be together and assume you know everything." I turn around and march down the porch steps, feeling like a zombie. "Tell Noah we'll move tutoring to my house. Give me ten minutes, and then you can send her over."

"Elena, wait."

More tears fall as I make my way across the street, ignoring Grant as he calls my name.

"Please, Elena." He catches my wrist when I reach my porch. "Don't go. Talk to me."

"Talk to you?" I spin around to face him. "*Now* you want to talk?"

"I didn't know—"

"You didn't ask."

"I didn't think—"

"No, you assumed you knew me, and you disregarded me and my feelings." I yank my arm out of his grip. "And I won't be with someone who treats me like that."

I walk inside my house, close the door in his face, and then I collapse onto the floor and cry.

"I'm going to ask you a question, and I don't want you to lie to me."

I close Noah's textbook and give her my full attention. "Okay."

"I mean it. If you're going to lie to me, then just tell me you can't answer the question. I'd rather that than a lie."

"I won't lie to you. What's going on?"

Noah drops her pencil onto my kitchen table. "Are you and my dad in a fight?"

My stomach twists. "Honestly, I don't know if you can call it a fight."

She throws up her hands. "I knew it. I knew something fishy was going on."

"I'd rather you talk to him about it first. I don't want to upset him."

"Oh, he's already upset." She rolls her eyes. "He's been in the worst mood these past few days, snapping at me and yelling at Romeo for no reason. Now I know why."

I grimace. "I'm sorry. I feel like it's my fault."

She leans in. "Len, what happened?"

I run my fingers through my hair and blow out a long sigh. "You're going to have to ask your dad."

"He's not going to tell me anything, and you know it." She lets out a frustrated growl. "I knew there was a reason you bailed on tutoring twice this week."

"It won't be forever." My eyes bounce around the room as I try to come up with a way to explain this for a fourteen-year-old. "Give it some time."

"Time." She clenches her jaw, and it's uncanny how much she looks like Grant. "You're avoiding him, and you need time. That sounds like a breakup. Were you dating?"

I shake my head. "No, we weren't dating."

"I would be so pissed if you were dating and you didn't tell me."

All this time, what even were we?

I thought we'd be more. I thought I meant more. It turns out we were nothing more than stolen kisses and secret love affairs behind Noah's back.

"I promise, we weren't dating."

"But...?"

"But...you should talk to your father."

"He won't talk to me. Ever. Anytime I ask him a question about my mom, he brushes it under the rug. He'll do the same with this." She throws her pencil at the table and it bounces onto the floor. "I hate this. Everything was going great, and now it's not."

"Hey." I lean in and rub her back in soothing circles. "Whatever is going on is between me and your dad. You and I still get to see each other. Everything is okay."

"No, it's not." Tears well in her eyes. "You don't get it."

"Help me understand. Tell me what you're feeling."

"I thought...I was hoping..." She wipes her eyes with the backs of her hands. "I want you to date my dad so you could be, like, my stepmom."

My heart falters in my chest. "You do?"

"Dad is happy when you're around. He listens to you, and he started treating me like I'm an actual teenager instead of a five-year-old." She sniffles. "And I liked having you there. I liked how it felt with you in the house. It felt like we were...whole."

I yank her chair closer to mine and swivel to face her. "You and your father are whole. Your father doesn't need a significant other to make your family qualify as a family. You two have each other, and that is more than enough. Stop looking at the things you're missing in your life. Appreciate what you have right in front of you. You don't have a mom. I didn't have a great dad. Your father doesn't have a wife. But none of that matters if you look at the people we do have." I grip her face and force her to look into my eyes. "And you will always have me in your life, no matter what house I'm in. Anything you'd want to ask your mother, you can ask me. I am here for you. Always. Do you understand?"

She nods before she flings her arms around my neck and hugs me with all her might.

I hold her while she cries, letting out as much teenage angst and confusion as she needs to.

It's only when she pulls back that I realize I'm crying too.

"I'm sorry. I didn't mean to make you cry." Noah reaches out and wipes away a tear rolling down my cheek.

"Since we're sharing secrets...want to know mine?"

She nods.

"After I married Neil, I found out that I needed a hysterectomy. Do you know what that is?"

"Is that when you remove all your baby stuff inside your body?"

"Yes. Your uterus is where the baby lives when you're pregnant. But I didn't have a healthy uterus. I had something called fibroids, and they were pretty large. I had a lot of complications, so I had to have everything removed."

Noah's eyes widen. "But now you don't have a place for a baby."

"That's right."

"You can't have kids now?"

"Nope."

"But you wanted to?"

I nod.

"I'm sorry, Lenny."

"You might not get to have a mom, and I might never get to have children. But me and you? We have each other." I take her hands in mine and squeeze them tight. "You are an incredible human. I see it, and your dad sees it. And he loves you with all his heart. Everything he does, every decision he makes—it's for you, Noah. You might not understand why he tells you no or treats you like a baby, but he always has your best interest at heart. So go easy on him. And remind him what a great dad he is, okay? He needs to hear it."

She nods. "Okay."

"Good."

I snag some tissues from the living room, and we wipe our eyes.

"Lenny, can I ask you one more question?"

"Of course."

"Do you love my dad?"

I pause, letting that word bounce around my head. "I think I was starting to."

"I think he loves you too."

My stupid hopeful heart attempts to leap out of my chest. "Whether he does or he doesn't, I'm here for you. Do you understand?"

She nods. "For what it's worth, I love you, Lenny."

"I love you too, kid."

17

GRANT

"What did you expect to happen when you sent this dickwad over to her house? God only knows what he said."

Jason scoffs. "Hey, I was a perfect gentleman to her. This has nothing to do with me."

I pinch the bridge of my nose. "I don't know what to do. It's been over a week, and she won't talk to me."

Mitch takes a swig of his beer. "Have you gone over there?"

I shake my head. "I've called and texted. But if she doesn't want to talk to me, I won't force her by showing up at her house."

That'd make me no better than her ex-husband, wouldn't it?

"Has she seen Noah?" Mitch asks.

"Yeah, she's still tutoring her. But they're doing it at her house instead of here."

"Give her time." Jason shrugs. "She'll come around."

"Once again, you're demonstrating why your generation sucks." Mitch shakes his head at him. "You need to prove to her that you're sorry. You can't just lie down and accept the fact that she doesn't want to talk to you."

Jason shoots him a dubious look. "Well, he can't make her talk if she doesn't want to."

"Women love romantic gestures. They eat that shit up. It's go big or go home when it comes to love."

While the two continue bickering, Trent glances at me from across the table. "You love her, don't you?"

Love.

I've had girlfriends when I was younger. I've had the words said to me, but I've never said the words to anyone. Not until Noah came into my life. She taught me what love truly means. It's unconditional. It's unwavering. It's unapologetic. You do what you have to do for the person you love, even if it hurts, because her needs come before your own. And when you love someone, that's all that matters —her and her needs.

"You pushed her away because you thought you were doing the right thing for her." Trent hikes a shoulder. "Isn't that what you do when you love someone?"

I swallow past the emotion in my throat. "She doesn't see it that way."

"Because *she* loves *you*. And she thinks you don't feel the same because you let her go."

I run my fingers through my hair, picturing her tear-stained cheeks as she left me standing on her porch. "I didn't want to let her go."

"So then tell her what you want."

"And what if it's too late?"

"You won't know if you don't try."

"He's right, Dad."

I turn around at the sound of Noah's voice, and the room falls silent.

She stands in the doorway, wringing her hands as she chews on her bottom lip. "I know you and Lenny are in a fight, but you can make up with her. You just have to tell her how you feel."

"And how do you know we're in a fight?"

She pulls out the chair beside me and turns it to face me as she sits. "I'm not an idiot, Dad."

"Did she say something to you?"

"She told me to ask you, which we both know is pointless because you never talk about anything with me."

"That's not true."

"It's not? Then tell me what's going on."

I glance around the table. "Look, the guys are over and—"

"Always an excuse! See? You do this every time." She shakes her head and crosses her arms over her chest. "But I'm not going to let you get out of it. You're going to tell me what happened between you and Lenny because she's my friend, and you hurt her. I know you're hurting too, and I can't stand to see the two people I care about feeling like this."

Irritation spikes in my veins, mostly because she's right, and when the hell did she get so smart? "The reason I don't have these talks with you is because you're fourteen years old, Noah. I don't want to worry you with grown-up problems."

"I'm worried anyway, so what's the point? Hiding it from me doesn't make it better. People think that older means wiser. But it doesn't. Older just means more stubborn."

"Can't argue with her there," Trent mumbles.

"Fine." I puff my cheeks and blow out a long breath. "You want to have an adult conversation? Let's have one. Jason said he liked Elena the night we were playing cards here. I told him to go over to her house and ask her out. She got mad."

Noah's jaw falls open. "Of course she got mad. She doesn't like Jason. She likes *you*."

I shake my head. "I told her that she's young and can be with someone her own age who she can have kids with and—"

"Oh my god." Noah's hand flies to her mouth. "That's what you said to her?"

"I didn't know she couldn't have children."

"She had to get a hysterectomy when she was with Neil because she had something that started with an F."

"Fibroids?" Mitch asks.

"Yeah, that. So now it's impossible for her to have children." Noah blinks. "She literally can't bear kids, and you told her to be with someone she can start a family with."

Fuck.

All the comments I've made to her about not being able to understand what it's like to have children…all the times I've told her that she'll know what it's like when she has kids of her own.

I had no idea. How could I? She never told me.

I lick my lips, my mouth feeling as dry as a desert. "But she never said anything."

"And you assumed like you always do, instead of asking her what she wanted or how she felt." She pops an eyebrow. "Just like you do with me."

"I do what I do because it's what's best for you. I'm your father, and that's my job."

"Maybe you don't always know what's best for me. You ever think of that? Maybe I'd like it if you asked me what I wanted. I'm older now. I have questions. I have opinions. I have feelings. I'm not the little girl who was afraid of the dark and believed in Santa. I'm turning into a young adult, and I want you to tell me about my mother so I don't have to sit here wondering what happened."

Emotions surge, blurring my vision. "I just want to protect you from the pain."

"I'm already in pain. Every time Mother's Day rolls around, or a teacher at school tells me to ask *my mom* to sign something, or my friends talk about their moms." Her bottom lip trembles. "You knew her. The least you can do is tell me about her."

She's right. She's telling me what she needs, and it's time I give it to her.

"Fine." I scrub my hands over my face. "I'll tell you as much as I can, but it's not going to make you feel better hearing this story—it's not all puppies and rainbows."

She straightens in her chair. "I can handle it."

I suck in a slow breath, choosing my words carefully. "I was out at a bar with Trent and some other friends we knew from college. Your mom started dancing with me, and that's how we met." I pause, looking up at the ceiling as if it has the strength I need to push out this next part. "I was drinking, and I wasn't thinking straight. I took her back to my apartment, and that's the night we made you. All I knew about her was her first name."

Noah scrunches her nose. "Eww. You had unprotected sex?"

My head hangs. "I'm not proud of it, and it wasn't a smart decision, but it brought you into my life, so I'd do it all over again if I had to."

"How did you know she got pregnant?"

"We'd exchanged numbers but didn't contact each other after that night. Then she texted me a picture of you nine months later on the day you were born and told me I was a father."

Noah clamps her hand over her mouth. "What did you say?"

"I was shocked. And since she was a stranger, I told her I wanted a paternity test." I look into her eyes, her irises the same dark-brown color as mine. "You're mine, kid. That one unsafe decision led to the best thing that ever happened to me."

Noah leans forward on the edge of her seat. "What happened to Mom after she had me?"

"We agreed to co-parent, but it became clear that she was addicted to drugs. I did everything I could to get her clean for your sake. But she wasn't well, Noah. She struggled with her mental health and she resorted to drugs to escape whatever she was feeling. So when she chose to leave you, it wasn't because she didn't love you. It was because she was suffering with something bigger than both of us."

"We learned about addiction last month in school." Noah stares down at her hands as she talks. "My teacher said it's hereditary… which means I could become an addict too."

"You won't."

Her eyes flick to mine. "How do you know?"

"Because you're a smart kid, and you won't let anyone pressure you into trying that shit." I point my index finger at her. "Not even Reese Paisley."

She averts her eyes again. "I don't understand why Mom would do drugs."

"Mental disorders take over your mind," Jason says. "And they make you do things you wouldn't normally do. My mom has bipolar disorder, and when she wasn't on her meds for a while, it got bad."

"Could I have a mental disorder?" she asks. "Are those hereditary?"

"They could be. But I think you would've exhibited signs by now." I lean forward and squeeze her knee. "And even if you did, we'd handle it together. You will always have me through all the good times and all the bad ones."

"You have us," Mitch adds.

Noah pauses, her eyes bouncing around the room as she absorbs everything I'm telling her.

"Does this make you feel better?" I ask.

"It helps, talking about it with you. Hearing the story from your experience." She hikes a shoulder. "It doesn't change anything, but it does make me feel better. I think the not knowing was worse."

I reach out and clasp her hand. "I'm sorry I kept it from you. You deserve to know."

"Just like Lenny deserves to know how you feel."

I never wanted to hurt Elena. I thought I was doing the right thing. Everyone says that if you love someone, set them free.

But maybe what she really deserves is someone to stand and fight for her.

Her father, Neil, even her mother are gone. And I pushed her away like she didn't matter. I made her believe that she wasn't one of the most important things in my life.

I run my fingers through my hair, pulling at the roots. "I messed everything up, huh?"

She nods. "But you can fix it."

"How do you know that?"

"Because I know she wants you to."

"Did she say that?" Mitch asks.

"No, but you're going to have to trust me on this."

"Okay, baby Yoda." I squeeze her shoulder. "I trust you."

18

ELENA

"Is that...is that my best friend?"

I roll my eyes as I step into Simone's house. "Ha. Very funny."

Simone wraps me in a bear hug. "I haven't seen you in weeks. I almost forgot what you look like."

"Let me look at you." I hold her shoulders out in front of me and set my gaze on her belly bump. "You're the cutest pregnant woman ever."

"Pretty sure all best friends are supposed to say that, but I won't complain if you want to give me a compliment." She gestures to her couch. "The pizza should be here in fifteen minutes."

I flop onto her couch and kick off my shoes. "Where's Randall?"

"He met up with the guys to watch the Giants game."

"How have you been feeling? Has the nausea subsided?"

"It's so much better than it was. After living on saltine crackers for days on end, I'm looking forward to pizza tonight." She waves a dismissive hand. "But I don't want to talk about morning sickness. How are you?"

"I'm fine."

She shoots me a dubious look. "Grant tries to hook you up with his friend and you haven't spoken in a week. Want to try again and tell me how you're really feeling?"

I heave a sigh. "I'm shitty. But I don't want to talk about it because there's nothing I can do about it."

Simone chews the inside of her cheek.

"What? What's that look for?"

"Look, you know I'm your best friend, and I'll support you through anything. But I wouldn't be your best friend if I didn't tell you my opinion."

I square my shoulders. "Which is…?"

"I think you're being a little too hard on him, given the situation."

My eyes widen. "What?"

"Yes, he was an idiot for trying to convince you to be with Jason. But his heart was in the right place, Len. He was pushing you away because he didn't want to stand in your way." She shrugs. "That sounds pretty damn romantic to me."

"Romantic?" My mouth hangs open for a moment as my brain tries to process. "How is it romantic that he didn't communicate with me or ask me what I wanted?"

Simone waves a dismissive hand. "Men don't communicate. Hell, half the women I know don't communicate either. But you have a fight, and then you learn how to communicate. You can't shut him out the second things get real."

"I'm not shutting him out. He shut me out. He made a decision on my life without even talking to me about how he felt or what he was thinking. He just decided I should be with Jason, as if I'm not a person with a brain in my head." I press my palm against my chest. "I'm not some damsel he can sell to the highest bidder."

"Or maybe he didn't want to put you in a position to choose between being with him or having a family, so he made the decision for you—a selfless act by a man who loves you."

"I can't believe you're saying this right now."

"Is it so crazy?" Her head tilts as she challenges me. "Grant has spent the last decade trying to protect Noah, and in turn, he has created this isolated life for himself. He finally meets someone he can fall in love with, but you're in a different stage of life than he is. To him, you don't have a family and you're still young enough to create one. Sure, he didn't know that you can't physically have children, but you're young enough to explore other options. If you two fell in love and started dating, only to find out that you both wanted different things later on, how would that affect Noah? All three of you would be heartbroken. So once again, he's putting your and Noah's needs before his own, and that makes me feel sad for him."

Tears burn my eyes as Simone's words set in. I don't want to hear her but I do. I understand what she's saying, and I didn't see it from her perspective before because I was too angry and too hurt.

"I just wish he would've talked to me about it before pushing me away," I whisper.

Simone reaches over and clasps my hand. "So, tell him that."

When the pizza arrives, we talk and we laugh, and it heals a small part of me inside the way a girls' night often does. But throughout the night, Simone's words bounce off the walls of my mind.

Is she right?

Should I talk to Grant?

Am I being too hard on him?

In the middle of an episode of *The Bachelor*, Grant's name lights up on my phone as if my thoughts summoned him.

"Oh, shit." Simone glances at the phone buzzing in my hand like a detonated bomb. "Answer it."

Nerves twist my stomach as I slide my thumb across the screen. "Hello?"

"Elena, is Noah with you?"

Fear spikes in my veins at the sound of his alarmed tone. "No. I'm at Simone's house. What's wrong?"

Simone leans closer to hear.

"Fuck." Something crashes before Grant speaks again. "She's missing."

I shoot up from the couch and shove my feet into my sneakers. "What do you mean, she's missing?"

"Hannah's mom picked her up and took the girls to dinner. It was getting late, so I texted her to see what time she'd be bringing

Noah home. She said Noah told her that she wasn't feeling well and that she asked to use her phone to call me to pick her up."

My eyebrows press together. "Why would she say that?"

"I don't fucking know, but no one has any clue where she is, and now I don't know what to do."

"It's okay. We're going to find her." I cover the speaker and mouth the words *I'm sorry* to Simone.

She waves me out the door. "Keep me updated."

I give her a quick hug, and then I bolt out the door. "Where did they go to dinner?"

"Houlihan's."

I glance at the time on my screen as I swing myself into my car. "I can be there in twenty minutes. Stay at the house in case she shows up."

"I can't just sit here waiting for her."

"Someone needs to be there when she walks through that door."

He's quiet for a moment. "And what if she doesn't?"

"We'll find her, Grant." I peel out of the driveway. "Call Hannah's mother and ask to speak to her daughter. Maybe her friends know what happened."

"Why would she lie like that?"

"I don't know, but we'll figure it out. Something had to have upset her to make her want to leave dinner with her friends."

"If this has something to do with that Reese girl, I swear—"

"Let's not jump to conclusions. Let me focus on driving, and I'll let you know when I get there."

"Elena…"

My heart wrenches in my chest. "It's going to be okay, Grant. There will be an explanation for this, and Noah will be safe. Trust me."

"How do you know?"

"Because she has to be."

"Be careful driving. Don't speed."

"I'll call you as soon as I get there." As soon as I end the call, I hit the steering wheel, letting out my frustration. "Fuck!"

Worst-case scenarios flash through my mind at warp speed.

Please let Noah be okay.

My entire body relaxes in relief when I pull into the parking lot at Houlihan's and spot Noah sitting on a nearby bench.

I jump out of the car and run toward her. "Noah!"

She meets me halfway and slams into me, eyes wide with tear-streaked cheeks.

I hold her tight. "Are you okay? What's going on? Your father is worried sick."

She pulls back, and anger twists her dark features. "He lied to me."

My head tilts. "What? What are you talking about?"

"Please don't pretend like you don't know. I need you to tell me the truth."

The truth? About what?

"Noah, what are you talking about?"

"I need you to see something." She storms into the restaurant, dragging me with her. We weave through the crowded bar to get to the tables in the back past the bar.

Noah's eyes dart around the room until finally they settle. "There. The waitress."

A woman with brown hair tied back in a ponytail saunters from table to table. She's definitely older than me, but I can't judge by how much.

My head tilts. "Who is that, Noah?"

Noah holds up one of the photos we looked at together on Black Friday while we were decorating for Christmas. "Now tell me you didn't know about this."

"I...how...why..." I sputter, trying to make sense of it all as my eyes flick from the photo to the woman.

Why would Grant tell us that Noah's mother died when she didn't?

"Wow." Noah's eyes widen. "He didn't tell you either."

I shake my head and swallow past the dry lump lodged in my throat. "There has to be some logical explanation."

Noah lets out a bitter laugh. "Because he's an asshole who lies."

"No. That's not true."

"Yes, it is. All my father does is lie about things and says he's protecting me. But in reality? He's doing it because he's a coward. He can't look me in the eye and tell me the truth."

"Hold on. Stop jumping to conclusions." My feet move before I can stop them. "Wait here."

Noah hides behind a tall plant, her eyes glued to the slender brunette woman taking a table's dinner orders.

I wait for her to finish, and then I step in front of her. "Excuse me. Are you Barbara?"

Don't ask why Barbara was the first name to jump into my head.

The woman smiles as she taps her nametag. "Sorry, I'm Tara. I don't know of a Barbara who works here."

My heart falls to my feet.

Tara.

Noah's mother.

"Can I help you?" she asks.

"I'm so sorry." I force a fake laugh. "You look like someone I used to know. It's…uncanny."

She shrugs. "I get that a lot. I must have that kind of face."

"Yeah, I guess so."

"Well, have a good night."

I don't know what else to do or say in the moment, so I let her walk away and make my way back to Noah.

I give her a small nod. "It's her."

"I knew it." Noah balls her hands into fists. "I'm so mad at him."

"We need to go home and talk to him. See what he has to say."

She shakes her head. "I refuse to go home. I can't even look at him right now."

I grip her shoulders. "We need to hear him out. Then you can yell and get mad and say whatever it is you want to say."

"How are you so calm right now? He lied to you too."

Sadness pricks my chest, but I push it aside for now. "Because I can't get angry until I hear all the facts."

"Nothing he says is going to make this okay." A tear rolls down Noah's cheek. "He said my mother was dead, but she's standing right there, and I had to find out when I was with all of my friends.

I had to pretend to get sick in the bathroom and tell them that my dad was coming to pick me up because I couldn't face them and explain what was happening."

Maybe talking to Grant when she's this upset isn't a good idea. If I can calm her down, maybe she'll listen to reason later.

I pull her in for another hug as her arms lie limp at her sides. "Come on. I'll take you to my house, and we can figure out what to do from there."

I shoot a text to Grant while I'm on the way home with Noah, but he calls me immediately.

She has her eyes closed with her head against the window, so I reject his call and type out a quick text when I get to a red light.

Me: Use my spare key under the mat and let yourself into my house.

Me: I have Noah but she's very upset and she won't come home if she knows you're there.

Grant: What the fuck happened?

Me: Exactly what you'd think would happen when you lie to your daughter and tell her that her mother died when she's actually alive.

I shove my phone back into my purse and let out an exasperated sigh.

I'm angry, hurt, and confused...but it's not about me right now. It's about Noah. She's old enough to understand this and if she wants to be mad at her father, she has every right to be. This kind of secret could break them.

I can't let that happen.

I pull into my driveway a few minutes later and take Noah's hand as I lead her into the house.

Grant rises from the couch in the living room as soon as the door clicks shut behind us.

Noah yanks her hand out of mine. "What is he doing here?"

"He's your father and—"

"You tricked me." She points a finger in my face. "You said we could talk about it and figure out what to do, but you called him behind my back. God, why does everyone always have to lie to me?"

Grant steps toward her. "Noah, what the hell is going on?"

"What's going on? Remember that random stranger you banged fourteen years ago and then told me she died? Surprise! She's alive."

His eyebrows press together. "How do you know that?"

"Hannah's mom took us to Houlihan's for dinner tonight. Imagine what it felt like to see the woman I thought was dead as my waitress."

His face pales. "How do you know it was her?"

"Because I saw her, Dad! Ask Lenny. She talked to her."

Grant's eyes flick to mine. "What did you say to her?"

"I pretended that I thought she was someone else and asked for her name." I chew my bottom lip. "Her nametag said Tara."

"And then what? Did you tell her about Noah?" He whips his head to his daughter. "Did you talk to her? What did you say?"

His hands are shaking, and his eyes are wide. He looks scared shitless.

"Grant, no one said anything to her, and that's not the point." I place my hand on his shoulder. "Please try to calm down so we can talk to you."

Noah shakes her head. "How could you lie to me about something like that? You made me believe that she was dead. Do you know how sick that is?" She covers her mouth with her hand to muffle a sob. "Was anything you told me real? Was she even an addict?"

He scrubs his hand over his jaw. "Yes, she was an addict. And she did try to commit suicide. She was a mess, Noah. She couldn't be in your life. I had to protect you."

"The only thing I need protection from is you and your lies!"

My heart rips out of my chest seeing Noah so distraught, but I don't know what else to do. Right now, they need to talk it out.

Grant moves toward her, but she steps back. "Don't touch me. I want you to leave."

A strangled noise leaves his throat. "I didn't know anything about your mother when we met or the life she led. I didn't know she was an addict. I'm the one who brought you into this world, and I needed to protect you. And that meant keeping you away from her. I'm sorry, but I—"

Noah cuts him off and turns to me. "Lenny, can I please stay here tonight? I really don't want to go home."

I glance at Grant. "I-I don't mind if it's okay with your dad, but I think you should—"

"He doesn't get to tell me what to do. Not after pulling this shit."

"Hey." Grant stabs his chest with his finger. "I know I lied to you, but I am still your father, and you will still treat me with respect."

"Respect goes both ways, Dad. You don't respect me enough to tell me the truth, so why should I respect you when all you do is lie to me?"

His fists clench and unclench. He's trying so hard to keep his composure when I know he wants to fly off the handle and carry her back to his house and lock her in her room.

"Maybe you both need some space to cool off and think." I squeeze Noah's shoulder. "But eventually, you're going to have to face what your father did and go home."

Without a word, she spins around and stomps upstairs.

Grant and I wait until we hear the slam of the door rattle the walls.

"I'll do my best to calm her down, but it might take some time."

Grant's shoulders droop as he lifts his watery eyes to mine.

I want to console him. I want to hold him and tell him that we'll get through this together. But I can't do that. Between the shock and the broken heart I'm still mending, and the crying girl upstairs…

Right now, I have to focus on Noah.

Instead, I offer him this. "I can't say whether I would've done anything differently had I been in your shoes. We do what we think is right to protect the ones we love."

He nods and then shuffles toward the door, wordless and lifeless.

And I let him walk back to his house.

Alone.

19

GRANT

My front door opens, and Romeo and I both spring from the couch. "Noah?"

My mother's somber face comes into view. "I'm sorry, honey. It's just me."

"What are you doing here?"

She shrugs off her coat as she walks into the living room and lays it over the arm of the couch. "I got a phone call from my granddaughter this morning."

"What did she say?"

"She called to ask if I knew the truth about her mother, and I told her I did."

My mother is the only other person who knows the truth about Tara.

I slump back onto the couch and dig the heels of my hands into my tired eyes. "I fucked up."

"No, you didn't."

"She hates me now."

"No, she doesn't."

"I've never seen her like this before. Whenever she gets mad at me, she stomps away and locks herself in her room. But she won't even come home."

"She just needs some time. This is bigger than a tiff about her curfew."

I let out a humorless laugh. "All this time I've been trying to keep her from feeling pain, and I'm the one who hurt her the most."

My mother lowers herself onto the cushion beside me, and Romeo sets his head in her lap. "I know you're feeling guilty about lying to Noah, and I know she's angry with you. But that doesn't mean what you did was wrong."

"What?"

"Being a parent means making tough decisions. Children won't always like the choices their parents make. Hell, they rarely ever like them. But we make these decisions in spite of what they want because it's our job to keep them healthy, happy, and safe. And your decision to keep her away from Tara is what has given her this beautiful life."

I shake my head. "Noah doesn't see it that way."

"And she won't until she's older." She clasps my hand. "But sweetheart, Noah isn't truly angry with you. She's angry at Tara, and she's going to lash out at the only person she knows she can lash out at."

"No, Mom. She's mad at me. Trust me. She made that very clear."

A slight smile curves her lips. "Do you remember when your father and I went on a cruise when you were little? I think you were five or six years old."

"When I stayed with Nan and Pop?"

She nods, and her smile widens. "You had so much fun with your grandparents that week. Every time I called to check on you, you were at the zoo or the movie theater or eating ice cream. But when your father and I came back from our trip, do you remember what you did?"

I shake my head, eyebrows pushing together as I try to recall that distant memory.

"You refused to talk to Nan for two weeks."

My head tilts. "I don't remember that."

"Oh, you were so mad at her. She'd come over for dinner and

you'd pretend she didn't exist. She'd ask to play with you, and you'd yank your toys away and tell her to leave you alone. She was absolutely heartbroken."

"Why though? Why was I mad at her?"

"You weren't. You were mad at me—and your father, for leaving you. But you couldn't take it out on us because you were so happy that we'd come back from vacation. You displaced your anger and took it out on the one person you knew you could. Nan was the one you felt like you could treat badly and get away with it, because you knew she'd love you no matter what."

Understanding settles into my bones.

"Noah might be angry with you for lying, but she's really angry with Tara for abandoning her. That pain runs deep, and since she can't take it out on Tara, she's taking it out on you because she knows you won't ever leave her. She's going to hurl it all at you, and you're going to take it. We carry the weight from the pain of our children, Grant. It's what we do. Nothing hurts us more than seeing our children hurting, even if we're the ones who caused it. But you did what you did to protect her from a very different life."

"What if Tara stayed clean? Maybe she got her act together after almost dying, and I deprived Noah of having a mother in her life."

"She didn't stay clean, sweetheart."

My eyes dart to hers. "How do you know?"

"Because I kept in touch with her parents."

"Why?"

"You had to keep Noah safe. And I had to keep you safe. When you called me from the hospital the night Tara tried to take her life, I was relieved that you wanted to take Noah away from her. But I needed to make sure that decision didn't come back to bite you in the ass. Tara's parents could've fought for partial custody of her. They could've taken you to court, and it would've drained your bank account and your energy when you needed to focus all of it on your newborn baby. So, I stepped in and offered to pay for Tara's rehabilitation to give her a chance to get clean as a show of good faith. Her parents were grateful for that. They believed that if Tara got clean, then she'd want to be Noah's mother. We had to show them that we believed that as well."

But she didn't stay clean.

"I also convinced you to send Tara's parents pictures of Noah throughout the years—which you were adamant about not doing, if you recall. You were furious with me for meddling in your business, but I knew it was the right thing to do in the long run." She pauses. "Tara has fallen off the wagon multiple times since Noah was born. Every time she tries to stay clean, she ends up back where she started. So you need to rest assured knowing that you made the right decision for Noah, whether she sees it that way or not."

I let my head fall back against the couch and exhale a long breath. "I don't know how to make this better."

"At this point, honesty is the best thing for her. Now that she knows, don't leave her in the dark with her thoughts. It won't be easy to tell her the truth, but she needs to hear it."

Tears sting the backs of my eyes. "It's going to break her heart."

"Then be there to help put it back together again."

I open my arms and pull my mother in for a long hug. "Thanks for coming, Mom."

"I wish I could say I came for you, but the real reason I'm here is to meet that lovely woman Noah is staying with."

A dry laugh rips from my throat. "I'm surprised you waited this long to say something."

She nudges me with her shoulder. "Who is she?"

"Her name is Elena. She lives across the street."

She arches an eyebrow. "If you're entrusting her with Noah, then she must be more than '*Elena who lives across the street.*'"

Warmth seeps into my chest. "She is more."

"Oh?"

I glance at my mother out of the corner of my eye. "I'm in love with her."

Mom claps. "Hallelujah! I thought I'd die before I got to see you fall in love with someone."

"You had a lot of faith in me, I see."

"Honey, I knew it was going to take a miracle for you to find someone who could put up with your stubborn, grouchy, set-in-your-ways attitude."

"It's not exactly like that."

"Why not?"

"I might've pushed her away."

Mom tilts her head, wearing that all-knowing expression mothers tend to have. "So, pull her back in."

"You say it as if it's easy."

"No, honey. Love is never easy. It's anything but." She leans closer. "Which is why it takes a lot of effort."

I nod. "I planned on fixing it until this whole thing with Noah happened."

"But you called Elena for help, and she came running."

I nod again. "She did."

"You made her think you didn't want her. Now it's time to show her that you do."

Elena

I TAP my knuckles against the doorframe. "Can I come in?"

Noah nods without lifting her eyes to mine from my bed. "It's your room."

I was hoping she'd be feeling better after sleeping on it, but she seems sadder today. Quieter. And I don't know if that's better or worse than anger.

I lower myself onto the edge of the bed. "Do you want to talk about anything?"

"I'm kind of talked out after last night."

"I get that." I stroke her hair as she scoots up against the headboard. "You feel like eating anything special for lunch? You barely touched the pancakes this morning."

"I do want something actually."

"Anything. What can I make for you?"

The whites of her eyes are bloodshot as she lifts them to meet mine. "I want you to take me back to Houlihan's."

"Oh, Noah. I don't know if that's—"

"Please, Len." Her bottom lip trembles. "I need to do this."

And in my heart, I know she's right. Her father has been fighting her battles for her, and he kept this major secret from her. She needs to confront Tara on her own. She needs answers, and they're the kind of answers her father can't give her.

"Fine. But I'm telling your father what we're doing."

She rolls her eyes. "Can you at least wait until we're on the way there so he can't try to stop us?"

"Deal."

Once we're on the way, I tap out a text to Grant.

Me: Noah asked me to take her to see Tara.
Me: She needs to do this.
Grant: OK

It took a lot for him to type those two letters, and I'd be lying if I said I wasn't proud of him for it.

I know it's killing him to be away from Noah. But Grant has come a long way from the angry, controlling man he was when I met him. His growth is important for both him and Noah.

And a small, selfish part of me wonders if he's capable of growing for me too.

When I pull up to Houlihan's, Noah turns to face me in the passenger seat. "You can stay in the car."

"Not a chance, baby girl." I yank on the handle and swing open my door. "I'll wait inside."

She walks around the front of the car and clasps my hand. "Good, because I'm really nervous."

I squeeze her hand. "It's okay to be nervous. Say what's in your heart. And whatever the outcome, I'll be right here with you."

"Thanks, Lenny."

I sit at the corner of the bar with a clear view of the dining room. Noah finds Tara talking with a few of the other employees at the waitress station. My stomach ties itself in knots as she takes the last few steps closer.

Dammit, I wish I could hear what they're saying.

Noah's back is to me now, but I can see Tara, so I try to make out what's happening based on her expression.

If that were me, I'd reach out and hug my daughter. I'd be shocked and amazed that she found me. I'd be caught off guard for sure. But I wouldn't be standing there looking cool as a cucumber with my arms hanging at my sides like Tara is right now.

Please be a decent human being.

Tara shakes her head, and then Noah spins on her heels and makes a beeline right for me. As she gets closer, I spot the glistening trails of tears on her cheeks.

I jump to my feet. "Noah, what happened?"

"We shouldn't have come here. Let's go."

I catch her arm. "Wait. Hey, look at me. What did she say?"

"Please, just take me home." She swallows a sob. "I want to go home."

Oh, hell no.

I dig into my coat pocket and hand Noah my keys. "Go start the car. I'll be out in a minute."

I square my shoulders and head for the main dining room.

Several waiters shoot me questioning glances as I march over to Tara, but I pay them no mind.

"What did you just say to that little girl?"

Tara's head jerks back. "Excuse me?"

"You said something to her, and she ran out of here crying. So I'll ask you again: What did you say to her?"

"I'm in the middle of my shift." She tries to move around me, but I step in her way.

"I'm not going anywhere, and I don't care if I make a scene."

Tara lets out a long sigh and smooths her hand over her ponytail. "The kid came at me, talking about me being her mother and asking where I've been for the last fourteen years. She was loud, and she wouldn't leave me alone. So, I told her: I'm no one's mother, and I'm not looking to be."

Adrenaline courses through my veins. "Y-you said you didn't want to be her mother?"

"Look, I made a stupid mistake fourteen years ago, and if I could go back in time and undo it, then I would. But I can't."

My mouth hangs open. "You *told* her that?"

"What else was I supposed to say?" She lifts her hand and lets it fall and smack against her thigh. "I didn't want to lie to her and make her think this was going to be some fairy tale reunion."

"You didn't have to lie to her, but you could've let her down gently. You could've said…literally anything besides what you said to her!" My jaw clenches as I force my breathing to even out. "She's a kid, and she just found out that her mother is alive after fourteen years. She's in shock, and she's confused."

She scoffs. "That's her father's fault."

I ignore the jab at Grant. "She just wanted to know you…to hear that you didn't want to abandon her like you did all those years ago."

Tara shakes her head. "I can't give her what she's looking for."

"You can't, or you won't?"

"Both. Now you and your little family need to leave me the hell alone."

Disbelief slams into me. "She's your daughter. Don't you care at all?"

A short man in a white button-down shirt with black slacks walks over to us. "Is everything okay here? Is there anything I can help you with, ma'am?"

I stare at Tara, searching for some sliver of humanity inside her. A sign of remorse. A modicum of understanding. But she gives me nothing.

"You know what?" A tear streams down my face as my lips quiver. "You don't deserve to know her."

I spin around and slam right into Grant's chest.

He engulfs me in his arms, holding me tight as he sets his eyes on Tara. His icy glare says everything his words don't.

TRICK OR TRUCE

I clutch his jacket like a lifeline, and Grant ushers me outside.

When the cold air hits us, he turns to face me. "You okay?"

I let out a disgusted noise from the back of my throat. "I cannot believe that woman. It's one thing to not want children. But who tells a child that you don't want them? Who looks her in the eyes and says that? God, I could strangle her."

"There's a reason it wasn't hard to cut her out of Noah's life, and it's because she didn't want to be a part of it. Forget about her. We have to be here for Noah and help her get through this."

"How are you the calm one right now?"

"It's like a weight has been lifted off my shoulders. I've been carrying around this lie for so long, wondering if and when this day would come, wondering if Tara would ever show up on our doorstep and ask to be a part of Noah's life." He hikes a shoulder. "Now that it's over, we can move on."

"And what about everything Tara said to her?"

Hearing something like that has to damage a kid permanently. I know the nasty things my father said to me growing up left scars.

"If she's willing to go, I'd like to take her to therapy." He glances at his daughter through my windshield. "I think I could use it as well."

I nod. "I think that's a great idea."

"Remember what you said to me? People are going to come in and out of her life, and some people are going to hurt her. But she has me, and she has my mother, and she has you. All this love has to count for something."

He's right. No matter what bad things she's experienced in her life, she'll always have a support system to help her cope.

Noah will always be loved.

Another tear drops down my cheek. "Let's take her home."

Grant

When Noah's mad at me, she locks herself in her room. When she's sad though...she curls up in my bed with Romeo.

That's exactly what she does when we get home from Houlihan's.

Elena and I slip into bed on either side of her with Romeo resting his head on Noah's leg. We lie there, holding on to her in the silence for a while.

To my surprise, Noah is the first one to speak.

"You didn't tell me the truth about her because you knew she didn't want me."

My chest aches. "I don't think she's in her right mind, Noah. Addicts can't think like we do. The drugs alter their brain chemistry. I went to the first ultrasound with her and noticed the scars from old track marks on her arm. When I brought it up to her, she swore she'd stay clean during the pregnancy, and as far as I knew, she did. She was clean when I met her, so I didn't have a reason to believe otherwise. But after she gave birth to you, she fell right back into old patterns and her drug use got worse. Only, I didn't know it.

"I went to pick you up from her apartment one day, and I could hear you crying from inside. She wouldn't let me in, so I broke down the door to get to you. There were empty pill bottles everywhere, and she was clinging to life on the floor. I called an ambulance, and on the way to the hospital, she flat-lined but they were able to revive her. If I'd gotten to her a few seconds later, she would've been dead."

I blow out a shaky breath through my lips. "I couldn't leave you with her again, Noah. If something would've happened to you, I wouldn't have been able to live with myself, knowing what I knew about your mother. I convinced her to sign away her rights to you the next morning."

A tear slides down Noah's face and falls onto the pillow. "Why did she even bother having me? That seems like an awful lot of work for nine months just to give me up at the end of it."

"Whatever the reason, I'm so glad she did because I have you." I lean down and press my lips against her hair. "I know I can't be your mother, but all I've ever wanted was to be the best father I could for you. And I hope that's enough."

Noah sniffles, and her hand wraps around mine. "You *are* the best father."

Emotion squeezes my throat. "You're not mad at me anymore?"

She shakes her head. "No more lies, Dad. I want you to be open with me from now on."

"No more lies. I promise."

And I mean it. Noah is growing up, as much as it kills me to admit, and she deserves to be treated like the young woman she is.

Noah glances over her shoulder at Elena. "Thank you for everything."

Elena chews on the inside of her cheek as sadness tugs on her features. "I just wish she would've been better for you."

"It hurts knowing that the woman who brought me into this world doesn't care enough to want me in her life. But I've been doing a lot of thinking..." Noah threads her fingers through Elena's. "You've been more of a mom to me than Tara ever was, and that's what I want to focus on. A complete stranger—who I stole from the first day we met—has my back and loves me."

Tears pour down Elena's face. "Always, Noah."

I let my own tears fall too. Because for the first time since Noah was born, I'm not worried about whether she has enough love or enough family. I'm not worried about the decisions I've made or what kind of person she's going to grow up to be.

Noah has everything she needs to live a happy, fulfilled life right here in this bed.

And so do I.

Noah falls asleep soon after our talk, so Elena and I tiptoe out of the room to let her get some rest.

My mother sets a cup of tea in front of Elena when we step into the kitchen. "It's so wonderful to meet you, Elena. I'm Grant's mother."

"It's nice to meet you too, Mrs. Harper."

"Call me Janine. Thank you for taking care of my granddaughter."

"And thank you for letting her stay with you last night and for what you did today." I rest my hand on her shoulder. "Thank you for everything."

"Of course. You know I'm always here for Noah." Elena wraps her hand around the mug. She doesn't smile. She isn't her usual sunshiny self. Her eyes have barely met mine since yesterday.

Fuck. All this time, I've been worried about Noah's reaction to finding out about Tara that I didn't think about how Elena might feel knowing that I lied to her too.

"I'm so sorry I lied to you about Tara."

She shrugs. "I understand why you did."

"Just because you understand doesn't mean it didn't hurt."

"It's all right, Grant. Don't worry about me." She stifles a yawn. "I'm actually going to get some rest myself. Noah didn't sleep much last night, and I was up talking with her."

I hate how cold she seems. Far away. I want to pull her against me and tell her how I feel. I want to feel her in my arms and know that she's mine. I want to breathe in her familiar sweet scent that I've missed so much over the last week.

But as much as I want her to stay, I know now isn't the right time to talk about us. It's been a crazy weekend, and I need to give her space.

Mom pulls Elena in for an embrace. "I hope to see you again soon."

After she leaves, my mother sniffles and dabs at the corner of her eye.

"Why are you crying, Mom?"

"I'm just happy to meet the person you finally decided to give your heart to."

As if I had a choice.

As if anything in this world could've stopped me from falling in love with Elena.

Now I need to figure out how to get her back.

20

GRANT

I stare down at my phone, willing it to vibrate with a response.

Me: Merry Christmas, Elena.

I texted her earlier this morning while Noah was opening her presents.

I know Noah misses her too. She's been holed up in her room reading on the new Kindle I bought her. It's always been just the two of us on Christmas Day since my mom started taking a holiday cruise to Italy with a widow support group a few years ago. But spending this holiday without Elena just doesn't feel right.

Which is why I burst into Noah's room. "Get dressed. I need your help in the kitchen."

Noah's head jerks up from the book she's reading in bed. "What?"

"We're bringing Christmas dinner to Elena."

Her eyebrows shoot up. "You want to bring the food to the nursing home?"

"W.W.B.D."

A wide smile spreads across her face. "Bruce Willis would definitely do that."

Elena's mother might not even remember who Elena is, and the thought of her alone on Christmas like that guts me.

"The only problem is, we don't know which nursing home her mother is at."

Noah snatches her phone off the nightstand. "Leave that part to me."

"All right." I glance at the clock. "I'll get started on peeling the potatoes. We leave in an hour."

Noah tosses her book onto the mattress and flings off the comforter. "*Operation: Get Elena Back* is officially underway!"

"THIS PLACE SMELLS FUNNY."

I elbow my daughter in her ribs. "Lower your voice. Don't be disrespectful."

"Sorry." She shifts the cooler from one hand to the other. "There. One-forty-six."

"Hold on, kid." I step in front of Noah. "We have to knock. We can't just barge into the woman's room."

I peer through the few inches of space between the open door. Elena is sitting in a chair with her back to me, facing her mother's bed, watching her as she sleeps.

I wince from the pang in my heart.

This is her Christmas.

Noah cranes her neck to see over my shoulder. "You did good, Dad. She's going to be so happy to see us."

I sure hope so.

I tap my knuckles against the door, and Noah walks into the room ahead of me.

Elena's head whips around, her eyebrows pulling down in confusion as she stands. Her eyes flick from Noah to me and to the bags we're carrying.

Then she covers her face with her hands, and her shoulders begin to shake.

Noah drops the cooler and rushes over to her, wrapping her arms around her midsection. "It's okay, Len. We're here."

Emotion strangles my throat. When did my little girl transform into this empathetic, caring, aware young adult?

"What are you doing here?" Elena sniffles and pulls back, wiping her eyes with the backs of her hands. "It's Christmas."

"We brought Christmas to you. It was Dad's idea, actually."

Elena's eyes meet mine, and I take a step forward. "Wasn't sure what kind of day your mother would be having, and I didn't want you to be alone."

Elena gestures to the bed. "Today's a bad day. She didn't recognize me when I walked in this morning, and she gave the nurse such a hard time. I hate seeing her like this."

Without hesitation, I engulf her in my arms, pressing my palm to the back of her head.

Noah wraps her arms around the both of us and holds us tight. "We love you, Lenny. We're your family too. We couldn't let you spend Christmas without us."

Family.

I guess we are. Elena has become one of Noah's closest confidants, despite how hard I've worked to keep everyone at arm's distance. And now, seeing how much love Noah has in her heart, I hate myself for keeping this from her.

I've had it wrong all this time.

So fucking *wrong*.

Isolating myself has isolated my daughter, and she's missed out on people and experiences and relationships.

She's missed out on seeing who I really am.

Who I could be.

Who I want to be.

With Elena by our side.

Standing here, holding the two of them in my arms…I've never felt surer.

Elena

I pull into my driveway and stifle a yawn as I kill the engine.

I stayed with my mother until visitation hours were over, hoping she'd wake up and be in a better mood so I could have even the tiniest bit of Christmas with her.

But she wasn't in a better mood.

I should be happy that Grant and Noah showed up with a delicious ham dinner, yet every time I think about the way he held me and told me I wasn't alone, it reminds me how alone I truly am.

No family of my own. No one to share the holidays with.

I hoist myself out of the car and drag my tired feet up the porch steps.

Then I let out a yelp.

Dark eyes blink up at me from my rocking chair. "Sorry, I didn't mean to scare you."

I swallow, willing my heart to stay inside my chest as it thrashes around. "What are you doing out here? It's freezing."

Grant rises from the chair. "I was hoping we could talk."

"Look, I appreciate what you did for me today. It was thoughtful and sweet, and I was so happy to spend the day with Noah." I hike a shoulder. "What more is there to talk about?"

"I'd like to talk about us. You haven't returned any of my calls, aside from everything that happened with Noah and Tara."

"What more is there left to say? You think I should be with someone my own age. I got your message loud and clear, Grant. And after the day I just had, I really don't need to rehash it all over again."

I stick my key in the lock and twist, but Grant covers my hand with his. "Forget everything I said."

My traitorous heart slams against my chest, screaming at me to hear him out.

"Please, Elena."

I spin around to face him, my chest brushing against his as he cages me in against the door. "Why did you come today?"

"Because I couldn't stand the thought of you spending Christmas without me and Noah."

"So you felt bad, is that it?"

"No, that's not it." His eyes pierce through mine. "It's because I miss you, and I can't go another day without seeing you. Please let me come in so I can make things better."

"Well, maybe it's too late to make things better." I arch a bratty brow. "Maybe Jason is on his way over right now. Maybe I took you up on your offer to date your friend."

He tucks a strand of hair behind my ear, amusement reflecting in his gaze. "Give me five minutes, and when Jason gets here, I'll leave."

"Fine." I push open the door and step aside as I wave my arm in front of me. "Five minutes."

I shrug off my coat and toss it on the back of the chair as I round the small table in the kitchen. I lean against the counter and cross my arms, bracing myself for whatever Grant is about to say.

Grant stands in front of me, resting against the opposing counter so we're face to face. "I'm sorry I hurt you, and I'm sorry I pushed you away. But I didn't do it because I wanted to. I did it because I thought it was the right thing to do. I did it because I want you to be happy, to have everything you want in life—everything you deserve."

"And you didn't think I could have that with you?"

"I didn't want you to regret it. To regret me. I didn't want to be the person who holds you back. You said it yourself that some people aren't meant to stay in your life forever, but they're meant to teach you a lesson. I don't want to be your lesson, Elena. I want to be your everything. Your present and your future. I didn't want you to tell me in five years that you were leaving because you wanted a family that I couldn't give you. I didn't know…I didn't know that wasn't an option for you. I hope you can see that my intention was never to hurt you. I was willing to hurt myself and let you go if that's what you wanted."

Simone was right.

"I understand why you did what you did, Grant. I just wish you would've talked to me about it instead of shutting me out."

His Adam's apple bounces as he swallows. "Noah told me about your surgery, and I'm so sorry you're in this situation. It kills me to know that you can't have children because I know you'd have made the most incredible mother."

Tears well behind my lids as my throat tightens, and all I can do is nod.

"It might not mean much, and I know it's not the same, but for what it's worth…you're the closest thing to a mom Noah has ever had."

I suppress the sob that climbs up my throat. "I love her, Grant."

"I know you do. Watching her with you has been one of the greatest joys of my life." His eyes glisten like obsidian stones. "She loves you. And if I'm being honest, I've gone and fallen in love with you too."

Emotion surges in my chest as a tear rolls down my cheek.

He loves me.

Grant reaches out and clutches my face between his hands. "This time without you has made me realize something. Maybe you're my lesson. Maybe I'm missing out on the greatest thing in my life next to Noah because I've been too afraid to let you in. Maybe everything we've been through in our past has led us up to this very moment because you're supposed to be in my life to show me how to open up this damn ogre heart of mine and show me that the happiness you deserve? I deserve it too. So, this is me saying that you were right, and I was wrong. I shouldn't have pushed you away. I should've talked to you about the way I was feeling. And I should've told you I love you the moment I felt it."

I grip his wrists as he cradles my face. "Say it again."

"That I love you?"

"That I'm right, and you're wrong."

He chuckles and rests his forehead against mine. "I was wrong, and you were right."

I run my fingers through his hair and grip it at the roots. "But your heart was in the right place, and I love you for it."

"You love me?"

"I do."

Grant cradles my face in his massive hands and kisses my lips. "I love you, Elena. You've brought the light back into my life, and I want to spend the rest of it giving you everything you deserve."

God, that sounds so good.

"Well, your five minutes are up, so you'd better get going before Jason gets here and—"

Grant slams his lips against mine.

The force of his kiss takes my breath away. He claims my mouth like he owns it, taking what he wants, tilting my chin and parting my lips with his tongue as he dives inside to search for mine. Every nerve ending in my body comes alive, sparking with heat and desire.

Our hands are frantic, unable to stay in one spot for too long like we can't get close enough. With a growl, he picks me up and plops me on top of the counter, gripping two handfuls of my ass as he pulls me against him. I wrap my legs around his waist and cling to him, winding my tongue around his and moaning into his mouth.

"I'm sorry, Elena." He gasps for air, speaking against my lips before his tongue sweeps back inside my mouth. "I'm so fucking sorry that I hurt you."

"This is all I've wanted, Grant. Just you."

"You have me. I'm yours."

My hands slip under his shirt, my fingertips roaming over the hard ridges of his muscles. "How long can you stay?"

"Noah is waiting for me to come back." He sucks my bottom lip into his mouth and releases it with a pop. "She was very concerned about our fight."

"What are we going to tell her now?"

He presses his lips to my neck. "That we've made up." His tongue skates along my skin. "That you forgave me." He nips at my collarbone. "That we're dating."

"Don't forget about the part where you were wrong, and I was right. That's my favorite part."

He smiles as he trails light kisses across my chest. "You can be right as long as I can have you."

21

ELENA

The doorbell rings, and excitement clenches my stomach.

But it's nothing compared to the way my body reacts when I swing open the front door and see Grant standing on my porch.

"Damn, Harper." A black dress shirt clings to his broad shoulders and chest, tapering down into the waistband of his dark jeans held together with a matching belt. His sleeves are rolled halfway up his forearms revealing lean muscle and veins. "You clean up nicely."

His eyes blaze a trail down my body. "So do you."

I turn in a slow circle, giving him ample time to stare at my ass in my cream-colored sweater dress. "I wore the boots especially for you."

"I appreciate the gesture." He steps through the doorway and snakes one hand around my waist, pulling me close to him. "I've been fantasizing about them since the day you showed up on my porch dressed like Black Widow."

I laugh. "You hated me then." I take the bouquet of red roses from his other hand and bring them to my nose. "These are beautiful."

"You're beautiful."

I tilt my chin. "Are we allowed to kiss, or do I have to wait until the end of the date?"

His dark eyes bounce between mine. "You're going to wait because if I kiss you now, we won't be going on a date."

I stick out my bottom lip and pout. "You're no fun."

"Oh, you're going to see just how fun I am." With a wink, he takes my hand and walks me out to his truck.

Noah is sleeping at Hannah's house tonight, so Grant insisted on taking me on a proper date before having a sleepover of our own.

He takes me to a restaurant that recently opened in town, and we're seated in a dimly-lit corner near a cozy fireplace.

My eyes bounce around the room at the giant abstract sculptures hanging from the ceiling. "It's beautiful in here."

"It sure is."

But his eyes aren't on the artwork. They're on me.

Heat creeps into my cheeks. "I didn't know you were such a romantic."

"I want to make you happy." He reaches across the table and covers my hand with his. "Which is why I went to the orthopedic today."

I lean forward. "You did? What did he say?"

"He gave me a prescription for an MRI. He said it sounds like there might be a bulging disk in my lumbar spine. I'd have to go to physical therapy for three months, and if that doesn't work, then he wants to try an injection."

"I know you don't want to do any of that, but the physical therapy might help."

He nods. "He also gave me a bottle of CBD gel. He said it's good for inflammation and can help with the pain when it flares up."

I squeeze his hand. "I'm so happy you went. I bet Noah is happy too."

"She's been bugging me to go for the last year."

"She's a smart kid. You should listen to her more often."

He glances at his phone. "I know she'll be fine at her friend's house tonight, but I hate it when she doesn't sleep at home."

"It's hard letting go of that control. But if anything goes wrong, she'll call you. I trust her."

A smirk curves his lips. "You trust the candy thief?"

"It's crazy how things turned out, isn't it?"

His thumb strokes the top of my hand. "It sure is."

Grant pulls into my driveway after our date and walks behind me on the path leading to my house.

I dig into my purse for my keys, unlock the door, and step inside.

But Grant remains on the porch.

I extend my hand. "Come on."

He clasps my hand and yanks me back outside, wrapping his arms around me as I stumble into his chest.

I crane my neck to look up at him. "What's wrong?"

"I don't want you to think you have to invite me in." He brushes my hair away from my face and presses his lips against my cheek. "We don't have to rush. I'd be very happy kissing you good night right here and going home if that's what you want."

"What I want is for you to come inside and undress me." I tilt my chin and brush my lips against his. "You were a perfect gentleman the whole night, Grant. But once we enter that house, I don't want a perfect gentleman."

"No?" He drags his nose along my neck, inhaling deep at the spot I spritzed perfume earlier. "You want the mean old ogre?"

"You know I do."

"Then you'd better run," he snarls as he pretends to feast on my neck.

I squeal and scamper into the house, bolting for the stairs. He kicks the door shut behind him and runs after me. At the top of the stairs, he catches me and tosses me over his shoulder as he stalks down the hallway.

"Grant, you're back!"

His teeth sink into my ass. "It's fine."

When we get to my bedroom, he sets me down and steadies me in front of him. I sway, smoothing down my hair that's sticking up in all directions. My chest heaves as I catch my breath.

"You are the most beautiful thing I've ever seen." He clutches my face and presses his lips to my cheeks, my eyes, my forehead. "Absolutely fucking beautiful."

I reach up and speak against his lips. "I want you so bad."

He grips my jaw in one massive hand and sweeps his tongue inside my mouth. He kisses me slow and deep, taking his time when all I want to do is rip our clothes off and feel him inside me.

He drops down onto his knees and slides his hands up along my thighs, crawling under the material of my dress. I pull it up and over my head and fling it across the room.

"These boots stay on," he commands. He trails kisses along my inner thigh, making his way up to my thong. He places a gentle kiss to the thin cotton, making my knees buckle. Then he hooks his thumbs around the strings on either side of my hips and rips it off my body.

I gasp and a shiver dances down my spine.

He sits back on his heels and gazes at my swollen glistening skin before running his thumb through my wetness. "Goddamn. You are perfect."

I grip his hair and jut out my hips. "Grant, please."

He tosses one of my legs over his shoulder and grabs two handfuls of my ass as he leans in. His hot breath sends goose bumps flying over my skin. Dark, molten eyes flick up to mine as he runs his tongue along my pussy, groaning his approval.

He laps me up with long, maddeningly slow strokes of his tongue, watching me from under his dark lashes. As the pleasure mounts like a wave, my hips move faster. Holding onto his hair, I rub myself on his tongue, relishing in the feel of his scratchy beard on my sensitive skin.

Grant curls a finger inside me, and my moans get louder. "Oh fuck. That feels so good. Yes, Grant. Right there."

White-hot heat explodes as my body shakes, and I call Grant's name over and over again. He groans in satisfaction from watching me come, his dark eyes wild and wide.

After my release, my legs buckle, and my body goes limp. Grant stands and takes all of my weight as he lays me on the bed behind us. He kisses his way up my body and slides his hand between my back and the mattress to unclip my bra before tossing it like a nuisance. His tongue swirls around my nipple, sucking it into his mouth and releasing it with a pop, turning to give the same attention to the other.

I reach up and claw at his shirt, frantic and fumbling with the buttons. "Take everything off, Grant. Now."

He tears off his shirt as he steps back from the bed. He unbuckles his belt and then yanks it out of his belt loops in one swift motion.

Fuck, that's hot.

He kicks off his shoes, shucks his jeans, and drops them to his ankles. His cock strains against his boxers, the outline of his impressive length making me wet all over again. I watch with rapt attention as he peels his boxers off his body and his dick bobs between us.

Grant crawls on top of me and devours me with a demanding kiss, sucking all the air out of me. I wrap my legs around his waist, digging my heels into his round ass so I can feel him against me.

"I need you inside me, Grant."

"The condom is in my jeans."

He turns away to look for where he threw them, but I pull his face back to me. "We don't need a condom, remember?"

Recognition flashes through his eyes, and they soften. "I haven't had sex in an embarrassingly long time. I'm clean."

"I got tested after I found out Neil had been with another woman. I'm good too."

He slides his swollen crown along my entrance, glancing down to watch. He's always so restrained, so in control.

I want him to let go.

I lift my hips, pushing his tip inside. "Fuck me, Grant. Fuck me hard."

With his eyes locked on mine, he plunges all the way into me.

"Oh god. Yes. Again."

He pulls out and slams into me, over and over, his control slipping with each thrust. His fingers dig into my hips, holding me in place as the sound of our skin smacking together mixes with the guttural sounds of his grunts.

I could come just from watching this beautiful, composed man unravel before me. His brows pinch together like he's in both agony and ecstasy at the same time.

He takes my ankles and hikes my knees up to my chest, and I see stars.

"Fuck, Elena." He pins my wrists above my head, rolling his hips as he drives into me. "You feel so goddamn good."

He pounds me into the mattress like he owns me, and I love every second of it. My clit rubs against his pelvis with his erratic thrusts, and soon I'm crying out his name as I come again. I clench around him, my pussy squeezing him, begging for him to give me what I need.

And he does.

Grant comes with a loud thundering roar and unloads inside me. We hold on to each other as we ride out our waves together until we're warm and sated and our bodies go slack. He showers me with kisses while we catch our breath.

He moves to pull out of me, but I stop him. "Wait. Not yet."

He arches an eyebrow. "What's wrong?"

"I want to bask in this moment for a few more seconds." I close my eyes and take a deep breath. "We're so connected, I don't want it to be over."

Grant brushes my hair out of my face and kisses my lips. "It's not over yet. This night is just beginning."

I grin. "You got more in you, old man?"

His head dips down and bites my neck. "I'm going to make you pay for that comment."

"I'm looking forward to it."

Grant

THE LIGHT of the moon streaks through the bedroom window.

I should be exhausted from our night, but I can't sleep.

I stroke Elena's bare back, trailing my fingers lightly over her soft skin, trying not to wake her. All I can do is stare at her. Touch her. Feel her. Breathe her in.

I'm so consumed by her, by this love. Feeling like this terrifies me, but it also excites me. For fourteen years, I've worried about every single thing. I never knew if I was doing the right thing for Noah, making the right choices for her. But right now, in this moment? With Noah having fun at a sleepover with her friends, and with the woman I love lying in my arms…I can't find a single thing to worry about.

I press my lips to her shoulder, and she stirs. "Grant."

My dick hardens at the sound of her sleepy moan. "I'm here."

"Can't sleep?"

"I'm afraid to." I wrap my hand around her belly and pull her flush against me. "I don't want to wake up and find out that this whole night was a dream."

She backs her ass into me. "This is real, baby."

I nip at the cusp of her ear, sliding my palm up to cup her breast. "I love you, Elena. I need you to know."

She turns her head to gaze at me in the darkness. "I love you, Grant."

I press my lips to hers as I grind my dick against her ass. "I want you, just like this."

She stays on her side and throws her leg over mine, spreading her thighs for me. "Fucking like rabbits for five hours straight wasn't enough for you?"

"That was fucking." I reach between her legs and rub her clit in idle circles. "This is making love."

Another moan flutters out of her as she moves her hips in rhythm with my fingers. She's warm and wet, and when I guide my dick inside her, her pussy wraps around me like it was made for me.

"I don't think I'll ever get enough of the way it feels to be inside you."

"I hope you never get enough of me."

"I've gone my whole life without you, and I had no idea how

much I was missing. But now that I have you, now that I know you, now that I know what it feels like to hold you and love you, to hear your laugh, to see you smile, to watch you with my daughter…I see just how much I missed out on, and I don't want to be without you ever again," I whisper in her ear as I pump in and out of her in slow and sensual strokes. "You own me, Elena. You have me completely. So I'll never get enough of you because the time we have left on this earth isn't enough for me to show you how much I love you, and I don't want to waste another second of it being without you."

She sniffles and reaches behind her to grab on to the back of my neck. I hold her in my arms and make sure she feels everything I'm trying to convey.

Mind, body, and soul.

EPILOGUE

ELENA

One Year Later

"Ready for dessert?"

I pat my stomach, full from Grant's delicious meal. "I don't think I can fit anything else in here right now."

Grant shoots Noah a wink. "I think she's going to want a bite once she sees what I made."

Noah claps from her seat beside me. "She's definitely going to want some."

I lean my elbows on the table. "Now I'm intrigued."

Grant rises from the table and pulls out a plate from the fridge covered by a silver dome.

"Oh, it's so fancy." I grin as I gaze up at Grant. "You really went all-out on this anniversary dinner."

We're counting Halloween as our anniversary since it's the official day we came into each other's lives.

Grant sets the plate in front of me and pulls off the top.

A small black velvet box sits in the center of the plate.

My heart falters as my hands fly up to my mouth. "Oh my god."

"Elena Donaldson…" Grant lowers himself onto one knee and reaches out his hand for Noah. She slides off her seat and kneels on the floor beside him. "I've fallen madly in love with you, not only because of the incredible woman you are but because of the way you love my daughter. I can't quite put into words how much that means to me. You've made a difference in her life, and you've changed mine forever. I never thought I'd find someone who could fit so perfectly into our lives, someone I'd trust as much as I trust you.

"You've pushed me, and you've helped me become a better man. You taught me how to open my heart when I didn't even know it was possible. You are the kindest, most caring person I've ever known. And I want to spend the rest of my life giving you everything you deserve."

My heart feels like it's going to explode out of my chest. I've never felt this way about anyone, this happy, this in love. Noah and Grant are my family now, and this makes it official.

"Lenny, will you marry my dad and be my mom?" Noah asks.

I fling my arms around each of them. "Yes! I love you both so much."

Noah reaches up to snatch the ring box off the table, and she hands it to Grant.

Grant flips open the top and holds out the ring. "If you want your own ring, I will buy you one. But I figured you might want to wear your mother's ring instead."

My mother.

My glistening eyes widen as I gaze down at the ring. "How did you get this?"

"Noah and I went to visit your mother. I called ahead to make sure she was having a good day. I asked for her permission to marry you, and she gave me the ring off her finger." He hikes a shoulder. "She said you always loved it."

"She remembered." I nod as he slips the ring onto my finger. "I want to keep this one. I love it."

Noah looks up at me, wearing the biggest smile I've ever seen.

Noah and Grant are everything I've ever wanted.

A family of my own.

"Well, I gotta go get ready. Hanna's going to be here soon to pick me up."

Grant's head snaps to the right. "You're leaving?"

She shrugs. "You're engaged. What else do you need me for?"

His mouth falls open, and he swings his gaze to me. "Do you believe this?"

Noah plants her hands on her hips. "What? Why are you being so dramatic?"

"I'm not being dramatic." His jaw works under his skin. "We just got engaged. I figured you'd want to spend the night with us. Have a movie night or something."

"Dad, everyone's going ice skating. I have to be there."

I bite my bottom lip to keep from laughing. "It's fine. Let her be with her friends."

He shakes his head as he pushes up off the floor. "Fine. Be back by nine."

Noah lets out a frustrated sigh. "No one leaves at nine."

"I don't want you to leave at nine. I want you to leave in time to be home by nine."

"Dad, oh my god! That's so unfair."

He crosses his arms over his chest. "So what time do you think you'll be home?"

She tucks her hair behind her ear, feigning innocence. "Eleven?"

"No. No way. You can't—"

I slip my arm into the crook of his elbow. "Who's driving you home?"

"I think Gianna's dad said he could pick us up."

"And will there be boys in your group?"

Noah scrunches her nose. "No, but I'm sure there will be boys from our school."

"Nope. No way," Grant says.

"Let her go." I squeeze his arm. "We'll celebrate our engagement ourselves."

Grant arches a brow like he can read my mind, which is completely in the gutter with the promise of alone time tonight.

"Fine. But eleven is my limit."

Noah squeals. "Thank you."

Then she bolts upstairs.

He shakes his head. "I really thought she'd want to spend time with us tonight as a family."

"She's fifteen. She wants to be with her friends. Don't take it personally." I press a kiss to his cheek. "Besides, now I get you all to myself tonight."

He wraps his hands around my waist. "So this was your plan, huh? Get Noah out of the house so you can take advantage of me?"

I chuckle. "Is it working?"

"Definitely."

"I actually planned on giving you a surprise tonight." I wiggle out of his hold and reach for my purse sitting on the counter. "Even though nothing is going to top this beautiful ring you just put on my finger."

"You didn't have to get me anything, babe."

"It's kind of for the both of us." I pull out a thin white envelope. "Open it."

He flips open the flap and pulls out the letter, his eyes scanning it eagerly to find out what it is. "You're selling your house?"

I nod. "The realtor thinks it'll be a quick sale since it's in such great shape."

"Are you sure that's what you want to do? I know you love that house and—"

"I'm sure." I slip the letter back into the envelope and toss it onto the table. "This is the only home Noah has ever known, and I'd never make you sell it just to move right across the street into mine. And even though Neil hasn't bothered me for the money, I want to cut ties with him for good. I don't want this looming over me."

"I get it. And you're here all the time anyway." He tips my chin and kisses my lips. "Are you sure this is what you want to do? You can always rent out the house and use it as an investment property."

"No, I want to sell it. I'm sure."

The thought of waking up in Grant's arms every morning and

having breakfast with Noah before we leave for school…it settles something inside me.

Regardless of what house I'm in, with Grant and Noah—I'm home.

Grant

ANOTHER YEAR LATER

GRANT

"My turn!"

My stomach coils in anticipation as Noah hands Elena her Christmas present.

Elena glances at me as she gives the rectangular box a playful shake. "I wonder what this could be."

Noah wrings her hands in her lap as she waits for Elena to tear open the wrapping paper.

Elena's eyes well with tears as she pulls out a beautiful crystal picture frame, complete with a picture of the two of them from last summer inside it.

"This is beautiful. I love this picture."

Noah smiles. "Flip it over."

I hold my breath as Elena turns over the frame and spots the white envelope taped to the back. She pulls out the contents and begins to read.

Noah watches Elena's expression, but I watch Noah.

The mood swings and slamming doors aren't as frequent as they used to be. We communicate a lot better than we once did. In what feels like the blink of an eye, she's sixteen years old, and I know it won't be long before she's driving and looking at colleges she's interested in applying to. As much as I hate that she isn't my little girl anymore, I love the new dynamic we have.

And I love that we've gotten to share these last few years with Elena.

Elena gasps as she flips to the next page of the letter, and her hand flies up to her mouth. "Oh my god. Are you serious?"

Noah flings her arms around her. "I want this as long as you want it."

"Of course I want this." Elena sobs against her shoulder. "Nothing would make me prouder than to adopt you as my own."

I wrap my arms around them both, and Romeo leaps onto the couch to be a part of our celebration.

After a teary embrace, Elena pulls back and looks at me. "Are you sure you're okay with this?" She holds up the adoption papers. "This is a big deal for you."

I lean in and peck her lips. "It's the easiest decision I've ever made."

She stares down at the letter, shaking her head in disbelief. "I've always wanted to be a mother. I never thought it'd be in the cards for me after everything that happened."

"I wish I could give you what you truly wanted." Noah swipes away her own tear. "I know you didn't carry me for nine months, and I know you didn't raise me when I was a baby. But you were meant to be my mother. I believe that in my heart."

I clasp Elena's hand. "And so do I."

"You not being in my belly doesn't make me love you any less." Elena squeezes Noah's knee. "I love you unconditionally, and I will always look at you as mine."

And I know it's true because she loved Noah before she held these adoption papers in her hand.

Going from *my* daughter to *our* daughter is something I never saw coming. I didn't expect to want it as much as I do now. Elena changed my perspective on life and love; she changed my relationship with Noah.

She changed *me*.

ANOTHER YEAR LATER

THE END

New to me? I always recommend starting with my emotional bestseller *Bring Me Back*

Looking for a series?
Read *Collision*
Book 1 in *The Collision Series*

Need something funny and light instead?
Check out my bestselling rom-com
Hating the Boss

Come stalk me:
Facebook
Instagram
TikTok

Want to be part of my warrior crew?
Join Kristen's Warriors
A group where we can discuss my books, books you're reading, & where friends will remind you what a badass warrior you are.

All of my books are FREE on KU:

<u>Collision (Book 1) – Reverse grumpy sunshine</u>
<u>Avoidance (Book 2) – Reverse grumpy sunshine</u>
<u>The Other Brother (Book3 – standalone) – Grumpy sunshine</u>
<u>Against the Odds (Book 4 – standalone) – MMA fighter workplace romance</u>

<u>Hating the Boss – RomCom standalone – Enemies to lovers workplace romance</u>

Back to You – RomCom standalone – Second chance workplace romance

Inevitable – Contemporary standalone – Bodyguard forbidden romance

What's Left of Me – Contemporary standalone – Best friend's brother grumpy sunshine

Someone You Love – Contemporary standalone – Forced proximity grumpy sunshine

Bring Me Back – Contemporary standalone – Next door neighbor cop romance

Dear Santa – Fake dating holiday novella

Heart Trick – Fake dating hockey novella

www.ingramcontent.com/pod-product-compliance
Lightning Source LLC
Chambersburg PA
CBHW070808090825
30790CB00006B/16